TITLE
A Mysterious Slayer
(Book Two)

Chapter 1

With just three or so hours rest added to his repertoire, seeing his office toward the beginning of today was less motivating than ordinary. Particularly following a night on the beverage and a moon light walk around the banks of the Hudson.

Jack looked through exhausted red eyes as he concentrated on the expanded guide of Lower Manhattan that was joined to his office data board. The guide had three red pins and three blue pins immovably squeezed into it. The red pins addressed the places where the casualties were most recently seen subsequent to leaving with a stunt. Bits of string from every red pin connected it to a relating blue pin that demonstrated the site where the bodies were unloaded.

The grouping of murders was in the Lower Manhattan region, except for Amber, who disappeared from Chinatown yet her body was found on the contrary side of the East River in Brooklyn. This area was as yet in closeness to the gathering of pins.

Jack's involvement in killers had instructed him that an enemy of different casualties would frequently subliminally perpetrate their wrongdoings inside their usual range of familiarity, that was, regions that were near where they resided or worked.

Jack realized that assuming the executioner was predictable with taking whores from New York's more unmistakable red light regions, his hypothesis proposed that Tribeca, or less significantly, further north in Greenwich Village could be the following targets. Murray Hill and Midtown showed up excessively far north to fit the example.

Jack gazed at the guide so eagerly he neglected to see Spence enter the workplace. 'Have you got something?' Spence inquired.

Jack looked at the moving toward Spence who held a bistro blended espresso in each hand. 'Figured you could do with this, Jobs.' He gave Jack an espresso.

'You're a lifeline Spence,' Jack said.

Given the night he had, Jack had not had the option to fit any morning meal in to his morning schedule, or even purchase an espresso and the unappealing espresso they presented at the station resembled sump oil.

Jack took a taste from his new hot espresso and stopped to relish the taste blast and warming advantages.

'I need to make a beeline for the Waldorf toward the beginning of today… You accessible?' Jack inquired.

'Cool, better believe it sure. I'm there,' Spence answered.

Jack stopped momentarily in a snapshot of consideration before he talked once more, 'Perhaps we can visit for certain eggs en route… I'm starving,' Jack said then tasted on his genuinely necessary espresso.

It was just a short drive to the Waldorf Astoria Hotel following breakfast. The Detectives showed up and were welcomed continuously shift Duty Manager, who presented himself as Duncan. He was a meagerly assembled, clean cut man with diminutive dull hair and over overstated camp quirks.

Duncan's hand shake resembled holding a dead fish; frail with no strength by any stretch of the imagination in his limp grasp. Jack was a man's-man and accepted that a handshake ought to be firm and solid. In Jack's reality you judge a man's person by the handshake he traded. Furthermore Duncan drearily bombed the person test.

When the Detectives' personalities had been affirmed agreeable to Duncan and the reason for their visit was clarified, he took the Detectives to his office found quickly behind the front counter. In the workplace he had electronic admittance to the lodging's visitor records.

Duncan tapped on his PC console with a genuine articulation of focus. Jack and Spence watched on.

From his PC records Duncan affirmed that Mr. Barry McDougall was a visitor at the Waldorf Towers for three evenings from fifteenth to the seventeenth.

'He looked at on the eighteenth,' Duncan affirmed. 'He remained in one of the Grand Suites - room 4514.'

At Jack's solicitation Duncan printed out the electronic security records that recorded each event when Mr. McDougall's room was gotten to through an electronic room key.

Jack inspected the printed list prior to understanding the postings just recorded admittance, not departure.

'Well obviously… ' Duncan started in his camp voice. 'Mr McDougall didn't need to swipe his key to leave his room… ' Jack and Spence traded a quiet look.

Jack filtered the records. 'The records for the sixteenth show that Mr. McDougall's room was gotten to multiple times. The previously was at 10.30am,' he said.

'That was likely house keeping staff setting up the room later the past visitors looked at,' Duncan clarified.

Jack gestured. 'The room was additionally gotten to at 1pm.'

'Mr McDougall is a VIP visitor and the 1pm access would
have been by the Duty Manger to guarantee Mr.
McDougall's room was all together before his appearance,'
Duncan said.

'I take it the 2.30pm access would have been McDougall
moving into his room… ?' Jack said.

'Right.'

'There was a further access at 6pm and one more at 9.15pm,'
Jack noted. 'Nothing further on the sixteenth.'

Duncan returned his concentration to his PC and started
tapping at his console. Later a fast pursuit he said, 'Mr
McDougall had a booking for one at 8pm in our inn eatery.
Records show… ' he said tapping more keys as he talked,
then, at that point, stopping to sit tight for the PC screen to
revive, 'he took that booking and his dinner was charged to
his room.'

'So it is reasonable for expect the 9.15pm passage was
McDougall getting back from his dinner,' Jack said to no one
specifically. He continued to peruse the rundown. 'Records
for the seventeenth don't show anything until 7.30am, when
his room was returned.'

Duncan again got to visitor records. 'Mr McDougall went to
for breakfast in the Astoria Lounge at 6.30am. I would say
the 7.30am access was him returning later breakfast,'
Duncan said.

Jack thought briefly prior to offering his contemplations.
'These records can't definitively exhibit McDougall went
through the night in his room later 9.15pm,' he said.
'Speculatively… ' he proceeded, 'in the event that he had left
the room whenever later 9.15pm, it wouldn't show on any
records. Assuming he didn't get back to the inn until 6.30am
for breakfast, the leave records wouldn't be any unique
would they?' Jack said.

'No, I assume not,' Duncan answered in his recognizable
delicate voice. 'Yet, where might he stay in the event that he
wasn't in his room?' Duncan asked gullibly.

'Where he remained isn't the issue at the present time,' Jack
said. 'It's assuming he remained here that evening.'

'Can you say whether Mr. McDougall garaged a vehicle when he remained during fifteenth - seventeenth?' Spence asked.

Duncan tapped at his PC keys stopping to screen the outcomes. 'Ok… Mr. McDougall's vehicle was Valet left. So to respond to your inquiry – yes,' He said in his plain campness.

'Is there CCTV film of the 45th floor lobby outside McDougall's room?' Jack said.

'Indeed there is.'

'Shouldn't something be said about the carport… ? Are the sections and exits covered?'

'They sure are. As is the carport inside.'

'Would the recording actually be accessible from the sixteenth and seventeenth?'

'Sure would. They save the recording for thirty days prior to deleting. Assuming that you follow me respectable men I'll bring you down to the security room… They will actually want to address any of your inquiries in regards to surveillance camera film.'

The limited admittance Security Monitor Room was a little dim room about the size of the normal room. It was situated in the lodging storm cellar and was just open from the sub-level carport.

The brilliant light transmitting from the three twenty inch level screen screens gave diffused lighting to the room. Situated over the three screens were six more modest ten by eight inch screens, which were all alloted the different fixed cameras situated all through the inn, predominantly over the passageways and limited admittance regions.

The Security Room was for all time monitored by one security official who used a console and switch stick to work the skillet slant zoom cameras. The administrator could turn the cameras 360 degrees, zoom in and out and follow visitor action.

Utilizing the remarkable numbers doled out to each camera in the inn the administrator could enter the camera number into the console and call up any camera inside the structure to one of the bigger screens at the work area.

Each camera recorded day in and day out and all recorded film was carefully date and time stepped for security purposes, including all that was physically alloted to any of the three huge screens at the official's work area.

Racking units lodging banks of PC hard drives were situated in a room promptly nearby the screen room.

The CCTV film from the lobby of the Waldorf Towers 45th floor plainly showed the entryway to McDougall's room. The security official called up the recording from the sixteenth and quick sent it to the occasions recorded on the print out given by Duncan.

Film they checked on portrayed McDougall going into his room at 9.15pm and he didn't leave the room again that evening.

Film from the morning of the seventeenth showed him leaving his room at 6.25am and returning at 7.30am. The reality he was in his room all night excused McDougall from any immediate contribution in the homicides.

Jack asked the Security camera administrator to call up the carport exits for the morning of the seventeenth from 12 PM onwards. At 2am McDougall's vehicle was portrayed leaving the carport onto 50th Street. The proper camera was sadly excessively far away to recognize any facial elements of the driver. Quick sending through the recording, McDougall's extravagance dark Mercedes was recorded returning at 4.30am.

Jack lifted his eyes to Spence prior to asking the Security official, 'Did Mr. McDougall report his vehicle taken, altered, or any harm to his vehicle whenever during his visit?' Jack inquired.

The Security official tapped on his console to check his rundown of episode gives an account of his PC records. Subsequent to looking through a short rundown he prompted that there was no such report made by Mr. McDougall.

'Then, at that point, the vehicle's key must be utilized to access and drive McDougall's vehicle.' Jack rubbed a thoughtful hand across his chin stubble. DID MCDOUGALL GIVE HIS KEYS TO SOMEONE…? WERE HIS KEYS STOLEN AND RETURNED…? These were points he would have to clarify with McDougall.
Jack asked the security guard to call up the camera footage of the area where McDougall's car was parked, to see if they could identify a person getting into McDougall's car.

The Security Officer punched in the unique numbers for several cameras, calling them up one after the other to view their coverage, but none covered the area where McDougall's car was parked.

'It is impossible to cover every square inch of the garage by CCTV cameras,' the guard explained. 'The area where McDougall's car was parked within the garage was unfortunately in one of those few locations where the CCTV cameras do not cover: a blind spot…'

Jack rubbed his chin. From the review of footage no-one was seen approaching the car, yet the car was captured on video driving out of the parking space towards the exit. The footage suggested someone approached the vehicle from this apparent camera blind spot.

'That can't be a coincidence,' Jack mumbled. 'This person had to know where the camera blind spots were within the garage. Who had access to these cameras…?' Jack said. 'Who would know what coverage these cameras had?'

'Only Security Staff and Hotel Management have access to the monitor room to view camera footage, usually following the report of an incident,' the Guard said. 'Events such as a guest who had a trip and fall, a pickpocket theft, theft from rooms, a troublesome guest and guests collapsing from illness, such as a heart attack are all recorded for the protection of the hotel.'

'What if a car is Valet parked. Where are the keys kept?'

'Central Parking operates the Waldorf's Valet garage parking. They will be able to help you with that but I'm pretty sure the keys are secured in a locked cabinet,' the Guard said.

'Does anyone from Central Parking ever enter this room and view CCTV footage?' Jack said.

'Um…' The Guard thought for a moment. 'On occasions the Supervisor might come in to check the garage footage if there was a complaint by a guest that their vehicle was damaged while parked.'

Jack nodded his understanding.

All relevant viewed CCTV footage was subsequently copied onto a disc and handed to Jack.

From the Security Room Duncan escorted the Detectives to the Central Parking Valet team located at the Hotel's 50th Street entrance. At that location he introduced them to the duty team supervisor, Brenton Wylie.

Wylie was an overweight twenty-eight year old male with flushed cheeks. He was articulate and appeared well educated.

It didn't take long before Jack realized that Wylie was full of his own importance. He was an over-confident egotist with an obvious, yet inexplicable superiority complex.

'All VIP guests of the Waldorf Towers, such as Mr. McDougall, use this discreet entrance off 50th Street where they have access to private elevators to their upper floors,' Wylie said. 'If they have a vehicle it is valet parked for them.'

'Do you know who parked Mr. McDougall's vehicle in the garage when he arrived on the 15th?' Jack asked.

'That responsibility would be assigned to someone from day shift, but I am unaware at this juncture as to who parked it,' Wylie said.

'Who decides where the car will be parked in the garage?' Jack asked.

'Parking space availability determines where a vehicle will be parked within the confines of the garage,' Wylie replied as if he was quoting verbatim a rule, or by-law. 'Once the vehicle is parked the keys are assigned to the corresponding hook in the key cabinet?' Wylie gestured to his right.

Jack scanned the vicinity. 'The Key cabinet...?'

'That's correct. The key cabinet,' Wylie said. 'It is organized to mirror the garage floor plan. For example, when a car is parked in a particular spot in the garage, say parking bay C7, the vehicle's keys are hung on the corresponding hook for C7,' Wylie explained.

NOT EXACTLY ROCKET SCIENCE. His cynical gaze moved to Spence as Wylie explained. His dislike for this person grew by the minute. Something about this guy rubbed against Jack's grain.

'OK...So WHERE is the key cabinet?' Jack was direct.

Wylie escorted the Detectives to a small inlet just east of the hotel lobby entrance and indicated a locked black wall-mounted cabinet about three feet by two feet. Jack watched as Wylie used a key attached to a retractable cord on his belt to unlock the cabinet. He opened the cabinet doors and proudly showed the Detectives how the keys were arranged in the cabinet.

The front door of the cabinet opened outwards to the right and a second internal door then opened outwards to the left, giving a winged effect to the cabinet that exposed a number of vehicle keys hanging on hooks.

'Who has access to the keys that secure this cabinet?' Jack said.

'Only the Shift Supervisors...and yes it is always locked,' Wylie added.

Ignoring his arrogance, Jack lifted his eyes towards the ceiling. There was a fixed camera mounted on the ceiling to record the key cabinet.

Wylie must've noticed Jack had observed the camera. 'That's right...' Wylie said in anticipation. 'We have the key cabinet recorded 24-7. After all, we are responsible for some very expensive motor vehicles.'

Jack's focus returned to Wylie. He paused briefly with a look of exasperation. He leaned in to Spence and whispered quietly an instruction for him to head back to the CCTV room and view the camera that recorded the key cupboard.

Jack addressed Wylie as Spence disappeared back down to the Security Room. 'Can you tell me who was in charge of the cabinet key on the night of 16th and into the morning of the 17th?' Jack said.

Wylie watched Spence depart. When Spence was out of sight Wylie removed a manila folder from the key cupboard. He ran his eyes over the contents of the folder containing records for past shifts.

His eyes lifted to Jack. His response was over-dramatized. 'It appears that I was working night shift during that period,' Wylie said.

Jack's eyes thinned as he regarded Wylie who was clearly trying to convince Jack his surprised reaction was genuine.

'Did you allow anyone access to the key cabinet, or give anyone Mr. McDougall's keys at any time during your shift on the 16th or 17th...?' Jack asked.

'Absolutely not.' Wylie was adamant. He punctuated his comment by slamming the manila folder closed between his hands. His tone suggested he was offended by the insinuation.

Jack's dislike for Wylie continued to grow exponentially. Something about this guy did not sit well with Jack. Jack responded firmly. 'CCTV footage from YOUR cameras shows

Mr. McDougall's vehicle being driven out of the garage via that exit there...' Jack motioned towards the closet garage exit, 'at 2am in the morning,' Jack said. 'They are the facts...The vehicle was seen on the footage returning at 4.30am,' Jack said. 'Yet you tell me the keys to his vehicle never left that locked cabinet.'

'Absolutely correct. Maybe his car was stolen...Maybe he gave someone his spare set of keys. I don't know,' Wylie said. 'Maybe you should ask Mr. McDougall,' he said.

'Oh we will...' Jack said. 'That you can be sure of.'

Although it was an emotion that was completely foreign to Jack's character, he decided that discretion was the better part of valor...at least for the time being. He allowed Wylie to think he held the upper hand, which in reality however a clever ploy by Jack.

He was confident there would be a round two of questions for Wylie and he opted to keep his powder dry for the moment.

Jack recorded Wylie's full name, address and contact details before he left to meet up with Spence down in the CCTV room.

Spence had just concluded his reviews and was exiting the room as Jack arrived. On their stroll back to their vehicle Spence updated Jack on his review.

'It looks like the camera was moved and then returned,' Spence said. 'Up until 1.54am the fixed camera recorded the key cabinet and its immediate surrounds uninterrupted. At

1.55am the recording shows that the camera was moved upwards, to the right so the key cupboard was no longer visible. The camera then recorded the white ceiling.

'At 4.35am the camera was returned back to its proper recording position covering the key cabinet. The camera does not capture who moved it on either occasion,' Spence said. 'I had the Security Officer check the entrance and surrounding external fixed cameras to see if he could identify anyone walking to the Valet inlet, but this too proved fruitless.'

'I don't like that fat prick,' Jack said. He held strong suspicions Wylie was possibly involved in some way. 'He knows more than he is letting on,' Jack added. 'You know he was the minder of the cabinet key on the night McDougall's car was driven out of the garage.'

'That would not surprise me at all,' Spence said.

During the drive back to the office Jack summed up what was learned from the Waldorf. 'The vehicle suspected of being used in the 3rd murder, McDougall's Mercedes, was taken from a car parking space that was conveniently out of view of any CCTV cameras. McDougall did not leave his room all night and quite possibly did not know his car was gone. This would be confirmed when McDougall was able to be interviewed.

'The driver of McDougall's car did not appear to try and conceal his face as he drove it out of the garage, presumably because he already knew the camera was too far away to distinguish facial features and characteristics.

'The camera that recorded the key cabinet was moved shortly before McDougall's vehicle left the garage, obviously to prevent the person accessing the vehicle's keys from being detected on CCTV footage.

'The camera was returned to its proper viewing position shortly after the car returned. The suspect driver was then able to exit the garage and avoid being caught on any CCTV cameras. He would require knowledge of the camera blind spots.'

'I forgot to mention...' Spence began. 'Just out of curiosity, I asked the Security Officer to bring up the footage for the same time from the night before and the night after the 17th. As expected the camera did not move at all during those shifts.'

Jack shook his head. 'Someone who works at the Waldorf with a knowledge on what the CCTV cameras depict is either our killer, or is in some way helping our killer...That you can be sure of,' Jack said.

'My money's on that fat prick Wylie,' Spence said.

'What we need now is for Barry McDougall to come in for a chat,' Jack said.

No sooner had Jack's words left his mouth when his mobile phone began ringing. Jack retrieved the phone from his inner suit jacket pocket and answered the call.

'Jack Head...Good...yep...that's right.' Jack looked across to Spence. His beaming smile suggested good news. 'OK, we'll be five minutes.' Jack disconnected the call and returned his phone to his pocket. 'Ask and you shall receive,' he smugly said, wobbling his head.

'Don't tell me money man McDougall is at the station now,' Spence said. Jack's smug smile was the only response Spence needed.

Both Detectives made their way up from the under building garage to the Police station front counter. Jack had a brief chat with the Desk Sergeant.

The Sergeant indicated a short plump gentleman wearing thick glasses sitting in the front row of chairs in the pubic waiting area. 'Says his name is-'

'Barry McDougall,' Jack finished the Sergeant's sentence.

The Sergeant smiled. 'Correct. Apparently you wanted to see him.'

'Thanks,' Jack said in his usual uninformative manner.

Jack made his way to the public waiting area. As he approached he caught the eye of McDougall, whose reaction suggested he anticipated it was Jack walking over to him.

'Mr. McDougall...?' Jack said.

McDougall stood to his feet. He smiled and extended his hand. 'That's right,' he said. 'You must be Lieutenant Head.'

Jack responded to the gesture and the gentleman shook hands. McDougall's hand was small, like a child's and plump. Jack's massive meat cleaver hand completely engulfed the smaller man's hand.

The painting hanging over the fireplace in McDougall's sitting room flattered how this guy appeared in real life. He was a short, corpulent man with the top of his balding head only coming up to Jack's chest. His male pattern baldness contributed to the appearance he was much older than his fifty-six years. The thick lens of his dark framed glasses magnified his eyes to twice their actual size. LIFE DOES NOT IMITATE ART IN THIS CASE.

'You met my wife yesterday, I think it was,' McDougall said to open the conversation, 'and she told me you wanted to see me.'

'That's correct,' Jack said. 'Thanks for coming down.'

Jack extended his hand towards the interior of the police station. 'If you could accompany me please,' Jack said as he began to walk towards a door situated to the side of the front desk. 'Did you drive down here this evening?' Jack asked as they walked.

'I did. I am on my way back home after I finish here.'

'Is your car parked out the front?' Jack asked.

'It is...Is that OK?'

Jack raised his hand. 'Yes, of course. It's fine.' Jack wasn't concerned about where McDougall had parked his car, he was interested in the car and what evidence it may contain.

Jack escorted McDougall to an interview room usually utilized for compiling witness or victim statements. These were separate rooms to the intimidating interrogation room. Spence met them in the room a short time later.

Jack explained to McDougall why the police wished to speak to him. McDougall confirmed that he WAS in New York City from the 15th to the 17th.

He also confirmed that he drove his black Mercedes to the WALDORF ASTORIA hotel where he stayed. He told Jack that his Mercedes was Valet parked when he first arrived and he did not use it again until he checked out on the 18th.

His business meetings were all in close proximity to the hotel so he traveled by foot, cab or subway.

Although diminutive in height, McDougall's voice was deep and assertive. He was in no way introverted or nerdy. He spoke with confidence and implied power in his voice that suggested corporate leadership and strength. He was clearly a clever and intelligent man that commanded respect. He was a short alpha-male personality and for some reason, Jack developed a liking to him.

McDougall confirmed that he did not lend his Mercedes keys to anyone, nor did anyone have permission to use his car while he was staying at the hotel.

He didn't notice anything different about his vehicle when he drove it after he checked out from the Waldorf.

He was incensed when he found out his vehicle had been driven by someone while he was staying at the hotel. He informed the detectives that he intended to make a formal complaint to hotel management.

He was horrified when told his car may have used in a homicide to transport a body. But the COUP DE GRACEwas when he was told that his vehicle was evidence in an ongoing homicide investigation and it would have to be impounded while forensics examined it for evidence.

'That was one week ago from what you're telling me...' McDougall said. 'There won't be any evidence in the car now...will there?' His confident tone faded with his uncertainty in these areas. 'I've been driving it all this time.'

'If you are the only driver of your vehicle, and you haven't taken passengers, or used the trunk much, then there could still be some vital evidence in your vehicle,' Jack said. 'We won't know until we take a look. We will also need to take some elimination fingerprints from you so we can identify any of your finger prints in your vehicle.'

A detailed statement was taken from McDougall. His black Mercedes was moved to the forensics' garage for examination while his elimination fingerprints were taken.

McDougall stood bent over the wash up area scrubbing his fingertips trying to remove the residual black fingerprint ink stains from his fingers.

He glanced over his shoulder to Spence. 'If my car is able to assist you in your investigation, then I don't mind, really,' he reassured. 'If you require my car for a day or two it's OK. I have some work I can do in the city. I just need my overnight bag from the trunk. I always carry changes of clothes in the event that my work causes me to stay longer than anticipated,' McDougall said.

Once all the formalities were completed Spence escorted McDougall from the back-of-house area to the police station front foyer. McDougall rejected Spence's offer for a lift anywhere. As they shook hands prior to parting ways, McDougall told Spence that although he was slightly inconvenienced by what had happened, he was happy to help in any way he could and hoped his information was useful to them.

Chapter 2

Jack was back at his desk after the weekend break. He held a fresh brewed coffee from his favorite café to help kick start his Monday morning. In preparedness for the new working week he flipped over the pages of his desktop calendar from last Friday's date to display Monday 26th March.

Over the weekend he tried to occupy his time constructively but the weather wasn't kind. Apart from his morning run, when you live on your own and are forced indoors by inclement weather, you tend to do a lot of deep thinking.

Despite the occasional ball game on ESPN, Jack wasn't a TV watcher, so he spent most of his evening hours with Rosie at her bar on Friday and Saturday night. When she closed up, he spent the nights with Rosie at her place. She was a great distraction for Jack. He didn't think about his work the whole time he was in her company.

With fresh coffees and Monday morning expressions on their faces the Homicide team gathered for their regular morning muster to discuss the status of the ongoing caseloads. The team meeting atmosphere was a relaxed environment; the only stipulation was that they were attentive.

Some Detectives perch themselves on the front edge of desks, others lounge back in their chairs, while some reclined with their feet crossed over on their desk.

The update revealed the teams were investigating a stabbing murder from a robbery gone wrong; a drive by shooting death of a fifteen year old boy; a drug related shooting homicide; a rape and murder of a thirty-five year old woman in her home and of course, the Cryptic Killer.

Each team provided a situation report updating the status of their investigations. One case was close to arresting the offenders. One team was conducting neighborhood door knock inquiries. In another, the case had only just been reported and then there was Jack's case. The oldest case and probably one of the least advanced of all current caseloads, which had more to do with the guile and sophistication of the Cryptic Killer rather than Jack's abilities as a Detective.

Just over a week and one half had passed since the last letter was received. All available leads had been followed and to this point, all inquiries had gone stale for Jack.

Peter and Debbie's visit to the remaining five luxury vehicles found one of the five could have been in New York on Friday the 16th, but their follow up inquiries later exonerated the owner and his vehicle.

Jack's inquiries therefore found that of the 19 black colored luxury vehicles in the New York area, only one was in New York on the 16th March: the vehicle owned by Barry McDougall.

If Desiree was correct in her observations, Jack knows this suggested McDougall's vehicle was used to pick up Amber from her street corner in the early hours of the 17th. What was not known was what happened after she was picked up. Did the driver drop her off after he had finished with her services and then the killer took her, or was the killer driving the car that picked her up...?

Jack's inquiries with Barry McDougall and the Waldorf Astoria suggested to him the strong possibility that the driver of the car WAS the killer and not just a John.

As expected, the forensic examination of McDougall's car failed to locate any usable evidence.

The killer had gone to a great deal of trouble to use a vehicle from the Hotel garage, most likely with the assistance of Valet staff who helped him avoid CCTV cameras.

He then returned the vehicle around 3 hours later. The time
the vehicle was away and the trouble taken to acquire it was
not consistent with someone taking the car JUST to pick up
a street hooker. It was time to follow up on something that
had bothered Jack.

He waited until 9am before calling the WALDORF
ASTORIAto speak to a Senior Manager. His call was put
through to a female who identified herself as Vanessa,
Executive Manager of the Hotel. Jack introduced himself
and advised Vanessa that he required some information
about staff who worked at the hotel on particular days.

Vanessa advised Jack she was happy to help 'New York's
finest', but unfortunately she did not know who Jack was. He
was after all just a voice on the other end of her telephone.
She did not know if he was in fact a police officer.

Jack commended her for her caution and suggested she look
up the telephone number for the police, dial it and ask for
Lieutenant Jack Head from Homicide. Vanessa said she
would do that straight away. Jack hung up his phone to
await her return call.

Fifteen minutes passed without a call. Jack started to
wonder if she had given him the slip. He prepared to drive
down there and meet her in person.

He removed his pistol from his top drawer and began to
prove his firearm. His desk phone warbled before he
completed the task. Vanessa had finally returned his call and
was satisfied he was THE POLICE.

'It is imperative that what we discuss remains strictly confidential,' Jack stressed.

'I understand,' Vanessa said.

'Good. Thank you. Now, do you have access to all staff rosters for the months of January and February…?'

'I do. Which employees are you interested in Detective?' she asked.

'At this stage I would prefer to give you some dates, and from that if you could tell me who was rostered to work the night shifts on those dates.'

Oh, Okay. What dates do you need?

'I'm looking for the Valet Supervisors who were rostered for night shift from the 18th to the 19th January and from the 15th to 16th February.' Jack could hear the computer keys being tapped.

'OK,' Vanessa said. 'Do you have a pen?'

'Go ahead.'

There was a further tapping of computer keys. 'Our records show that Brenton Wylie was the rostered night shift Valet Parking Supervisor for both shifts that you have inquired about.'

The news caused Jack to nod knowingly as he scribbled down Wylie's name, heavily underlining it several times. He knew there was something about that kid he didn't like and it wasn't just his annoying personality. The shifts Jack asked about, the ones where Wylie was working, were the dates of the Cryptic Killer's first two murders.

'So he was rostered for BOTHthose shifts?' Jack clarified.

'That's correct Detective.'

'Are you able to confirm that he actually WORKEDthose shifts? He didn't report in sick or swap a shift?' Jack asked.

'Yes, he worked both shifts,' she said. 'Do you mind if I ask why the Homicide police are interested in Brenton, Detective? Has he done something that I should be aware of?'

Jack provided his standard non-committal response. 'Not at this stage ma'am...We're just conducting inquiries.'

Jack wasn't aware if the first two murders were similar to the 3rd in that they involved the use of a car stolen from the Waldorf. But it started to appear like they did. He took a punt just to see who was working Valet and by coincidence, or otherwise, Wylie just so happened to be working on the same nights as the first two murders as well.

For the first time in the investigation Jack had a sniff of a suspect. But was Wylie directly involved in any of the three murders? Would it be possible for him to leave his post during a shift, commit the murders and then return unnoticed? It's possible, but was it likely?

Wylie could be providing the keys and moving the cameras to assist the killer steal the cars. But why? What's in it for him? And if so, this suggested he COULDknow who the killer was, or at least, be able to ID him. Could this be the breakthrough he looked for?

'Ah, when is Brenton next rostered to work, Vanessa?' Jack asked.

'What's today...Monday the 26th', she said answering her own question as she tapped on the computer keys. 'OK... he is on rostered days off at the moment...Ah...let me see...He's due back on...night shift on Saturday 31st', she eventually said.

Jack reminded Vanessa of the importance of his inquiries remaining confidential and he ended the phone call.

At this stage Jack realized that most of the information about Wylie was circumstantial, at best. He would definitely need to be speak to Wylie, but without evidence to prove Wylie was assisting the killer acquire vehicles, he risked Wylie alerting the killer that the cops were on to his car theft racket. And this would be detrimental to the investigation. This one had to be managed carefully.

After hanging up the phone Jack reclined back in his chair and locked his fingers behind his head. His eyes moved to the three faces on his whiteboard smiling back at him. His brow dipped and his eyes began darting. WAIT...IF WYLIE WAS BACK ON NIGHT SHIFT ON SATURDAY 31ST AND HE WAS SOMEHOW INVOLVED, IT WOULD BE INTERESTING TO SEE IF THIS WILL BE WHEN WE RECEIVE THE 4TH LETTER?

Jack and Spence decided to get some fresh air. The stuffy recirculated air in their office was tiring. Both men exited the building on foot and decided to take a stroll towards Chinatown, to see what's happening out on the streets.

The fresh air instantly re-oxygenated the blood flow to their brains. The day was overcast and the breeze was a little cool, but it wasn't as noticeable when walking.

As they neared Chinatown the smell of the cuisines from the various restaurants activated their hunger rumbles. A roadside hot dog vendor caught Spence's eye. He nudged Jack then pointed to the vendor. 'Hot Dog?' he suggested. Jack nodded in agreement.

As Spence approached the vendor he raised two fingers to the man. Jack peeled off and leaned his left shoulder against a light pole watching the steady flow of traffic pass by.

A female voice calling his name from behind broke Jack's traffic watching. 'Jack...?'

Jack pushed himself away from the light pole and turned to the voice. It was his ex-wife, Caitlyn. She held shopping bags in each hand. She smiled at Jack. 'I thought that was you...how ARE you...?' She approached him, elevated herself onto her toes and kissed him on his cheek.

'Good...I'm good. You...?' he asked. He was a little cautious not to show too much interest, for no reason other than the fact they were divorced and do not keep in contact. Plus he didn't want to show he still loved her. 'What brings you down here?' he asked.

Jack had only seen Caitlyn once or twice since the divorce. It wasn't a bitter break up. She still loved him dearly, but his job just kept them apart. It forced them to live separate lives.

They were able to part friends, as friendly as you can when you decide to separate. They just never kept in touch when she moved.

'I'm down here with work for the day, so I thought I would do a bit of shopping in my lunch break.' She lifted up her shopping bags.

'Are you still doing the Business Development Consulting...?' Jack asked.

Caitlyn smiled and rolled her eyes. 'Still doing it. I have some clients in New York City, which is why I'm here.'

Jack nodded his understanding.

Spence watched the interaction from the hot dog vendor. He knew Caitlyn well and often reminded Jack that he let that one get away.

'How are the boys?' Jack said, with a hint of melancholy.

'Oh, they're great...'

Jack couldn't remember the last time he saw his sons, but it would be several years. He thought about them often and he missed them greatly, but they were effectively estranged from him. 'Wasn't it Dan's 24th birthday last month...?' Jack asked.

'That's right.' Caitlyn smiled at him. She appeared impressed Jack remembered, given his years of forgetting everyone's birthdays. 'We all went out for dinner to celebrate.'

'That sounds great...' he said as his remorseful eyes fell heavily. His voice revealed a hint of disappointment and regret.

Caitlyn rested her shopping bags on the ground and removed her cell phone from her purse. 'Here...' she tapped on her mobile phone. 'These are some photos from Dan's dinner.' She turned the phone to Jack.

Jack accepted the phone and looked at the photographs. His expression was clearly one of mixed emotions. He was happy to see his boys again but he was saddened he wasn't part of their lives.

He silently viewed the photos of what was once his family. His interest firmly focused on his boys and how they have matured into fine looking young men. His feelings were bitter-sweet. They all looked so happy but he was not part of it.

'They look great. Thanks for that Lynnie.' He handed back her phone.

She smiled as she accepted it. 'They're both great boys, Jack.'

'What are they up to these days...?'

'Dan is doing the final year of his Masters in finance. He has his sights firmly set on Wall Street...' she smiled.

'Good for him… Doesn't hurt to aim high. Can be lucrative if he can get a foot in the door…'

'And Maxi is a consultant of sorts. He loves it. He floats between here and California doing contract work for different firms… Actually…' She checked her watch.
'I THINK he's in California at the moment. I don't get to see much of either of them these days.'

Jack nodded in response. He smiled as he watched Caitlyn proudly talk about their boys. 'That's great to hear…' Jack said.

He gestured towards Spence at the Hot Dog vendor. 'You remember Spence…'

Spence smiled and waved.

'Of course I do. How are you Doug?' Her customary greeting sounded genuine.

'I'm good Caitlyn.' Spence said. He smiled as he approached Caitlyn and kissed her on the cheek. 'Are you still up in Jersey…? Maplewood wasn't it…?' Spence was only making small talk.

'Maplewood, that's right.' She nodded.

Spence nodded and smiled. 'That's great.' He gestured towards the vendor. 'Excuse me, Caitlyn,' he said, 'it was good to see you again…' he said as he moved over to the collect the hot dogs.

'So how are YOU doing...?' Jack said.

'Well, I remarried. You knew I remarried, didn't you?'

Jack shook his head. 'No. No, I didn't know. Good for you,' Jack said. Even though he had no right to, it stung a little bit when heard the news she had remarried.

Caitlyn scoffed and rolled her eyes. 'Seems as though I'm not meant to be married, Jack...It didn't last. We separated six months ago,' she said.

'I'm sorry to hear, Lynnie,' Jack said. He lied.

'No it's all good. I live on my own now, well, with Dan when he isn't at his girlfriend's, but mostly on my own and I'm loving it,' she said.

'Good for you,' Jack said.

The friendly small talk had all but run its race. Awkward silent pauses started to dominate their chance encounter.

They both exchanged the standard, 'you're looking well' compliments to each other. Then came the 'it was great to see you again' comments.

Following a kiss on the cheek and a brief embrace, they parted ways. Caitlyn moved deeper into Chinatown and the Detectives opted to return to the office.

'Here you go big fella…get this into ya.' Spence shoved the hot dog under Jack's nose.

'Thanks buddy.' Jack took a large bite. 'Argh…ordinary dog,' he moaned.

Jack was more refreshed from the exposure to the fresh air as he strolled chomping down on his hot dog. But if he was true to himself, the true reason he felt better was because he bumped in to Caitlyn. It was so good to see her again.

His frame was silhouetted against the darkness as he slowly stepped his way down the dimly lit stairs that led down into the darkened basement. The sound of creaking timber treads was eerie against the darkness.

The man's eyes were firmly fixed on the small room at the foot of the stairs. A large slide bolt and padlock secured this room that was once used for storage but was now a place utilized for far more devious and sinister purposes.

After stepping inside, he clicked on a low wattage desk light hovering over his laptop. For the areas away from the desk, the dull light blended into the darkness.

In the fading shadows, the wall in front of him revealed a mixture of the grey and black shades from the collection of newspaper clippings pasted across the wall. Each clipping was a reference to the same subject.

Some of the news reports dated back as far as ten years, with others as recent as January this year. A number of the clippings had a large photograph under a large headline. Some clippings had small photographs. Others had just text articles but regardless of the format, they all have one thing in common; the subject of news article.

Each news article that lined the wall like a mosaic wallpaper was a report on New York Homicide Detective, Lieutenant Jack Head. Most were extolling his superior policing following the successful arrests and prosecution of violent murderers. Others were media interviews about the status of ongoing cases but one constant was, Jack Head.

The dates on each article suggested he had been collecting them for some time; over many years in fact. But why? Why was he so interested in what Lieutenant Jack Head had done, or how he did it?

Why did he collect the articles like a proud parent whose child's picture had appeared in the local newspaper? Was he recognising his brilliance as a Detective? Or was he a disgruntled previous collar with a revenge wish?

Seated at his desk, camouflaged by the darkness that extended to each corner of the room, his silhouetted body was hunched slightly over his keyboard as he typed.

The desktop light hovering over his keyboard cast dancing shadows across the laptop keyboard from his typing hands and reflected a blend of black and brown shadows up his face.

Moments of pausing in contemplation were followed by frantic typing. It was as though his fingers couldn't type his thoughts quick enough. Longer pauses from typing were used to consult nearby reference material before returning to his typing.

Once he had finished he saved the typed page under the Cryptic file name, "A WARNING TO PLAYERS". He smiled to himself, quietly pleased with his guile.

The man reclined back in his chair and extended his arms out horizontally to his side to stretch. He yawned, then opened the top desk drawer and slipped out a pair of latex gloves from a box and promptly snapped them on, wiggling his fingers into the extra snug fit.

With his gloves in place he loaded a single page of lemon yellow paper into his printer then printed the file from on his laptop screen. While the printer did its job he removed a standard business sized, lemon yellow envelope from a drawer.

Once the page was ejected he slid the printed document from the printer's tray and held it under the light to examine the print quality before proof reading the contents.

Satisfied with his work, he placed the single page onto the desk and placed the envelope into the printer document feeder to print the recipient's name and address.

After tri-folding the single page typed letter he slid it carefully into the envelope. A piece of clear Sellotape was attached to the envelope's rear flap to securely seal it.

He dropped the sealed envelope onto the desk in front of himself. He leaned forward onto his elbows and raised his eyes to the shadowed wall in front of him. His eyes scanned over the mass of dark and light grey shades of dimly illuminated newspaper articles. A devious smile emerged across his face. All he needed was a stamp and it was ready to be posted.

The man dragged off his gloves then removed his cell phone from his jeans pocket. He levered open the back cover and flicked out the small battery. He then gently slid out the SIM card, which he immediately replaced with another SIM he had sitting on his desk. He then reassembled the phone.

After the phone had methodically completed its system reboot he sent a text message.

"HOT DATE LINED UP NEED A SWEET RIDE. WHEN R U NEXT WORKING"

The reply text message was promptly returned. "COOL. SAT SUN MON TUE."

"GOOD. WILL B IN TOUCH," The man replied then quickly reversed his earlier actions and replaced the original SIM card back into his phone.

All was now in readiness. He now had his date. The desk light was extinguished and the small storage room once again stood in total darkness, secured by the slide bolt and the over sized padlock.

Chapter 3

Jack was at his desk when the afternoon mail was delivered. He spread the envelopes, knocking the pile of letters apart so he could see who they were from before deciding if he could be bothered to open any of them just yet.

An envelope with the familiar FBI logo with "PRIVATE and CONFIDENTIAL" emblazoned across it in red ink caught his eye. He nudged the less interesting envelopes out of the way to dig through the pile and lift that envelope.

Federal Bureau of Investigation, National Center for the Analysis of Violent Crime, Critical Incident Response Group, he read.

'Looks like the profile from the Feds,' Jack yelled to Spence.

Jack slipped on his reading glasses and ripped into the envelope. He swiveled his chair to the side so he could cross his legs in readiness to read the FBI's reply.

Spence strolled into Jack's office and slumped down in the visitor's chair at Jack's desk. He watched on as Jack read the letter to himself.

The Federal Bureau of Investigation's Behavioral Analysis Unit (BAU) has examined all available information in regard to your matters.

This included, CCTV footage, photographs of the crime scenes, autopsy reports, victims' profiles, police reports, and witness statements.

The resultant Psychological Profile and Behavioral Analysis has been provided and is not for publication or circulation to anyone outside your department.

Apart from the CCTV footage provided there has been no evidence provided to the FBI that would assist in determining the physical description of this unknown subject ("UNSUB").

The CCTV footage provided depicts a driver of the subject vehicle however there is no evidence provided at this time to suggest the driver of the vehicle is the unsub. The CCTV footage provided however suggests the driver of the vehicle is;

Adult male;

Caucasian;

Mid to late twenties;

The Unsub's Psychological and Behavioral Profile

Based on the case file information this Unsub has been classified as an "Organised Murderer". Organised murderers have advanced social skills, plan their crimes, display control over their victim using their social skills, leave little forensic evidence or clues, and often engage in sexual acts with the victim before the murder.

The strength required to snap the C2 and C3 cerebral Vertebrae suggests the Unsub is a male of considerable strength and power. Possibly has some form of training in unarmed subjugation.

Victims are all young-adult Caucasian female street prostitutes. This suggests the killer is most probably Caucasian.

The killings do not appear to be motivated by uncontrollable urges or desires. He kills his victims quickly which suggests a feeling of remorse towards them.

Although he is murdering prostitutes the killings do not appear to be targeted hate crimes against prostitutes. There is no evidence he participates in sexual intercourse with his victims; possibly hires them for oral sex as a lure before killing them. The lack of extreme violence suggests the murders are not because of the killer's feelings of inadequacy or impotency.

He does not despise them for their lifestyle – he shows some care in the way he lays out their bodies, which are intentionally not well hidden. He wants them to be discovered.

He has no interest in his victims; they are chosen at random because he views them as easy targets. Street prostitution is illegal therefore there is a reluctance among prostitutes to voluntarily speak to law enforcement and it is not unusual for them to get into stranger's vehicles.

The crimes are well planned. He has meticulous attention to detail. He acts alone because he needs to control his environment.

He is not concerned that his crimes follow a particular pattern.

He is of superior intelligence and well educated. He is a strong controlling personality with extreme self-confidence, possibly a superiority complex, or even narcissism.

Has a thorough knowledge of crime scene forensics and law enforcement.

He has a disregard for the law. Possibly has committed other crimes previously and never been held to account.

He is careful not to leave incriminating evidence at his crime scenes, but he leaves a clue for the police as to where he will dump the victim's body.

He is clearly confident the cipher he has employed in his letters is solid enough to stave off decryption, but he will have a contingency plan in case the letters are deciphered.

The time between killings is reducing.

He is growing in confidence with every attack. This may cause him to make mistakes.

This unsub will continue to offend until he is caught.

Modus Operandi and Signature

Signature

Prior to the perpetration of the murder, coded letters are sent to police with hidden clues that another death is pending; the method he will use to kill his victim and where the body will be dumped.

All his victims have been killed instantly by snapping their C2 and/or C3 Cerebral Vertebrae.

The absence of bruising or physical injury suggest the victims were not forcibly abducted.

Toxicology reports indicate the victims were not drugged.

The lack of defensive wounds on the victims suggest a surprise attack.

Modus Operandi

His MO is to steal luxury motor vehicles from a hotel car park, possibly assisted in some way by a hotel employee and he uses the vehicle to pick up a street prostitute and take her to a remote location and kill her.

The vehicle is then used to transport the body to the dumping site before the vehicle is cleaned internally and returned to the hotel before the owner knows it was gone.

All victims have been picked up from around the same general area in Lower Manhattan and with exception of one, the bodies were dumped in relative close proximity to where they were picked up.

This could suggest the Unsub is committing crimes within the comfort zone of an area within which he resides or works.

FBI records have not matched this MO to any known offender or suspect.

Disclaimer:

Psychological and Behavioral profiling is not an exact science and should only be used to assist in identifying possible suspects. The above psychological and Behavioral profile provided has been based on the limited information made available to the FBI Behavioral Analysis Unit. The discovery of further evidence or information when considered in its entirety may alter the outcome of this offender's profile.

'Any good...?' Spence asked when Jack lowered the letter.

Jack gently lobbed the letter towards Spence. 'Given the small amount of information we gave the Feds, it goes into a bit of detail...' Jack began, 'but, it didn't really contain anything we hadn't already considered.'

Spence lifted the letter and read it through. When he had finished he returned the letter to Jack. 'Doesn't help much at all, does it...? Nothing new,' Spence said. Like Jack, his expectations appeared to be also slightly deflated.

Jack copied the FBI letter in preparedness for distribution to his team members at the daily morning muster tomorrow.

Thursday afternoon in Washington Square Park was warm with an agreeable gentle breeze. The brilliant blue sky blended from cobalt blue to azure and was almost unhindered by the sparse coverage of small fluffy white cumulus clouds.

Most of the buildings surrounding the popular park belonged to New York University. The park was a very handy and popular place for students to meet and relax before, or after classes.

Light numbers of visitors to the park gathered around the large centrally located Washington's fountain, while others were posing for photos in front of the towering Washington's arch at the gateway to Fifth Avenue. Others simply passed through as a short cut to their destination.

Lawn areas bathed in sunshine were occupied by University students sitting in groups, or just taking the time out on their own to relax or read.

Shaded park benches around the perimeter of the square were filled by people choosing to sit and rest, or just soak in the ambiance. Other university students challenged their minds against one another in the park's outdoor Chess playing area.

For Emma Fisher the lure of the lush sun-soaked lawns of Washington Square Park was a pleasant alternative to the stuffy University library to read over her course notes.

She was casually dressed in her light grey baggy sweat pants and a sloppy fitting purple NYU hoodie. Her shoulder length strawberry blonde hair was tucked up under a baseball cap.

Her choice of clothing did nothing for her natural beauty and masked her femininity and her fit athletic figure.

She sat crossed legged on the lawn facing the direction of the fountain, with the sun on her back. Her elbows rested on her knees and her head was lowered as she focused on the reading material on the lawn in front of her.

Emma was a vibrant and attractive twenty-two year old senior studying her final year of law at NYU. Originally from Philadelphia where she grew up living with her mother, she moved to New York after high school to study a law degree.

After two years living in campus accommodation she decided it was time to move into her own apartment to maintain her privacy.

She saved enough money for a deposit and rent down-payment through her regular part time job.

Weeks of fruitless searching for an apartment did nothing to dampen her enthusiasm and eventually, her persistence paid off. She was fortunate enough to find the perfect apartment at reasonable rent on the 12th floor at PETER COOPER VILLAGE in STUYVESANT TOWN, East Village.

Her modern one bedroom apartment, complete with ebony finished timber floors and large windows, overlooked what she referred to as her MILLION DOLLAR VIEWS of the East River across to Northern Brooklyn.

At night the mesmerizing view across the river to Brooklyn was a tranquil sea of sparkling street and building lights that gently flickered against the darkened night sky.

Her apartment boasted a sizable kitchen, complete with all appliances, separate dining room and a large living room. Her huge master bedroom came complete with en-suited bathroom and walk in closet. She felt it was perfect and only a thirty minute walk, or twenty minutes by bus to NYU.

Emma lifted her eyes from her books and scanned the park as she took a refreshing drink from her water bottle. She noticed the breeze had cooled and the number of people in the park had noticeably reduced.

The shadows from the park's trees hand lengthened and now stretched towards the central fountain. The best part of the afternoon had passed and was giving way to the approaching evening.

Emma checked her watch. She raised a single eyebrow in surprise that 2½ hours had passed by since she first sat down on the lawn. She closed her books and packed them into her backpack.

She removed her iPad, booted it up and navigated to her INSTAGRAM Page where she read through her many news feeds and messages.

She then posted a new status to her loyal following to advise them she would be working tonight from 10pm and would love to catch up with anyone who happened to be in the area.

Emma then packed up her back pack and hitched a single strap over one shoulder. After a quick check of where she sat, she made her way across the park towards the bus stop on Fifth Avenue to fight for a seat with the evening peak commuters as she made her way home.

Jack and Spence spent the afternoon in Jack's office going over the Cryptic Killer case. They reviewed what evidence they had, what evidence was needed and they mapped out what avenues of inquiries remained.

Both men agreed that the Waldorf Astoria Valet Supervisor, Brenton Wylie is still an important piece of this cryptic puzzle.

Jack updated Spence on how earlier in the week he tried to contact Wylie on his mobile on three occasions but all calls went to Wylie's voice mail.

He left messages on each occasion however Wylie failed to return his calls. He suspected that Wylie was intentionally ignoring his calls, which only caused him to dislike Wylie all the more.

Not to be denied, on Wednesday morning Jack drove out to Wylie's home address in Brooklyn for a cold-call visit. His knocks at Wylie's apartment door went unanswered, suggesting nobody was home but his instincts suspected Wylie was refusing to open the door.

Jack made some inquiries with Wylie's neighbors who confirmed Wylie lived at the apartment alone. As far as they knew he was home. He had certainly not gone away anywhere for his days off. One neighbor said she passed

Wylie in the hallway about fifteen minutes earlier when he was returning to his apartment.

'I thought, fuck him,' Jack blurted, with his contempt for Wylie peaking. 'For ignoring me...I'll just drag him away from his work on Saturday night.'

'Sounds fair to me,' Spence said.

Both men had spent several hours concentrating as they reviewed the case file. Spence lounged back in his chair and clasped his hands behind his head. He glanced across the desk at Jack.

'I could go a REAL coffee right now,' Spence suggested.

'Good call,' Jack said. He removed a folded $20 bill from his shirt pocket and flicked it across the desk to Spence, like a casino dealer distributing a playing card. 'My treat,' he said as the twenty came to rest in front of Spence.

Spence beamed an agreeing smile, followed by a nod back to Jack as he scooped up the note from the desk and made his way to their favorite coffee shop.

Spence would only have been gone two minutes when Jack heard Spence's distressed voice call out from the Bull Pen. 'Jobs...You better get out here....now.' His tone was direct.

Jack emerged from his office. He frowned his confusion when he noticed Spence seated at his desk.

'What happened to the coffees?' he asked.

Jack's smiling expression instantly wiped. His eyes locked onto the lemon yellow envelope in Spence's latex gloved hand.

Jack stopped in his tracks, as if shot. His shoulders slumped. His face now mirrored the same expression of trepidation as Spence.

'Lemon yellow paper...' he said knowingly.

Spence nodded slowly. He tilted the envelope towards Jack to show the letter inside.

Jack rolled his eyes, followed by a shake of his head. 'What's that...two weeks...? He asked.

'Yep...fifteen days to be exact,' Spence said. 'The time between letters is getting shorter.'

Jack watched Spence carefully remove the letter from the envelope, then carefully open the tri-folded letter. Spence left the letter sitting on his desk. The fold caused each end of the letter to rise upwards like butterfly wings.

Jack retrieved two clear evidence bags from the supply cupboard and handed them the Spence.

Once the envelope and letter were safely sealed in the clear evidence bags, Jack accepted the letter from Spence. His questioning eyes scanned over the contents.

Letter number four had arrived. It was identical to the previous three letters. There was a literary quote, a number of Cryptic Clues and rows of numbers.

Jack remembered what Matthew Curry told him previously, so he looked closer at the cryptic clues. Just like the previous letter, this one also had some small dots and a hyphen inconspicuously positioned in the clues. 'If the killer was consistent, these would be the clues that revealed the coordinates for a library or similar location for books,' Jack said, thinking out loud.

Further examination detected dots and a hyphen in the string of numbers. 'They will be the coordinates to where the body would be dumped.'

Jack handed the evidence bag to Spence. 'Get a copy of the letter and then enter the originals into evidence,' Jack said. 'Then get the originals down to prints to get them analysed, ASAP,' Jack barked. 'My office when you're done Spence.'

Once Spence had left, Jack addressed the entire team, all of whom had witnessed what had just occurred. 'Listen up...' Jack began. 'Effective immediately...all your cases are on hold,' he said. 'This case is now our number one priority...You will all be required to help on this one...I will update everyone shortly with your tasks,' he said, then returned to his office.

Spence returned to Jack's office about fifteen minutes later having completed his list of assigned tasks. He flopped down into the visitor's chair opposite Jack and slid the copy of the 4th letter onto the desk. Jack didn't notice the letter. His focus was fixed on the whiteboard.

'The murders have gone from five weeks, to three weeks to now two weeks,' he said while staring at the whiteboard. 'The time between killings is reducing considerably.' The concern lines from a fortnight ago returned to Jack's face.

'But we've got Matthew Curry,' Spence said.

Jack scanned his desk. 'Where's the copy?' he asked. He saw the letter on the desk before Spence could respond. Jack lifted the letter and read the opening quote.

"THERE ARE TWO CLASSES OF PEOPLE IN THIS WORLD, THOSE WHO SIN, AND THOSE WHO ARE SINNED AGAINST; IF A MAN MUST BELONG TO EITHER, HE HAD BETTER BELONG TO THE FIRST THAN TO THE SECOND."

Jack looked across at Spence. Both men shared a glance that confirmed neither understood the significance of the quote. Jack accessed the GOOGLEsearch engine and typed in the latest quote. He rubbed his hands together while he waited for the results.

'OK.' Jack squinted while he read from the computer screen. 'According to this...the quote is by SAMUEL BUTLER.' Jack looked across at Spence. His mouth inverted and he shook his head. 'Do you know who that is?'

Spence shook his head. 'No idea...'

Jack's focus returned to the screen. 'Ah... it says here he was an English novelist...Another quote from an English writer,' Jack noted. He continued reading. 'He was born in 1835 and died in 1902.'

'Does it say there what book the quote is from, Jobs?'

Jack read from the screen. 'OK... it says here the quote is from the novel, "THE WAY OF ALL FLESH," he said. 'So it looks like we know the novel, next we need to get these cryptic clues answered so we can decipher the message.'

'Do you want to use Curry again, or the intelligence boys, given we know how to decipher the letter now?' Spence said.

Jack's eyes flicked to Spence as he sat back from his computer screen. He rubbed a thoughtful hand across his mouth. 'Who is most suitable...or qualified...?' Jack said, thinking out loud. 'The intelligence boys are law enforcement...Matthew Curry is just a clever kid...but still a civilian...' He said.

'But Matt knows exactly how to crack this cipher. He's already done it three times,' Spence said.

Jack nodded. 'I agree. I think we'll break protocol and use Matty...' Jack said. 'Time is of the essence and he'll be able to knock this over quickly. We just have to be sure he will maintain the confidentiality of what he reads.'

Spence smiled and nodded at Jack's choice. 'I agree.'

Jack's mind started to tick over. Spence obviously noticed his boss was deep in contemplation. 'What's on your mind Jobs?'

Jack flicked the stubble up the side of his face. 'If this letter is consistent with the others we have received...' Jack paused. His focus shifted to the whiteboard. 'We have forty-eight hours to stop him, 'Jack said.

Spence shrugged. 'Nothing new there Jobs.'

Jack's frowning focus shifted to Spence. 'Forty-eight hours from today would be what day...?'

'Saturday...' Spence said. He shook his head. 'Where you going with this?'

'When is that fat prick's first shift back from rest days...?' Jack asked knowingly.

Spence's eyebrows arched. 'Saturday night...' Spence said.

Jack nodded slowly. 'I don't think it is a coincidence Spence. The more I think about it, the more I am certain that Wylie is somehow involved. We just have to find to what extent.'

Jack checked his watch and noted that the business day was nearing an end. This meant office workers across the city would be bursting from their buildings, racing impatiently towards their nightly commute home. And that included Matthew.

'Get his work number from his statement and catch him before he goes home. I want him here tonight,' Jack ordered.

'I'm on it.' Spence jumped from his chair and exited the office.

About ten minutes later Spence leaned in through Jack's office door to inform him Matthew was on his way.

'What did you tell him?' Jack asked.

'Not much...Just asked him to come down to the police station before he goes home and stressed it was important...He seemed happy with that.'

Jack nodded and Spence was gone.

Jack dialed the Gnome's extension. He was not as concerned about contacting him this time. Jack felt confident that he was already ahead of the killer and with a bit of luck, they might be able to prevent this 4th murder.

The phone answered after two rings. Jack informed the Gnome that the 4th letter had just arrived. He updated the Captain on what his plans were and how he intended to try and prevent this next murder, including short term, bringing in Matthew Curry to have the letter cracked tonight.

The Captain offered some initial resistance on his decision to use a civilian in a murder investigation, but after a compelling argument from Jack as to why Matthew was more qualified, the Captain conceded that he probably was the best suited person for the job.

Jack reassured the Gnome that they knew a lot more and were in a much stronger position than when they received the 3rd letter two weeks ago. It was now up to Matthew Curry to crack this latest cipher - and quickly.

Chapter 4

With her bus approaching the intersection with 15th Street Emma pressed the "Next Stop" button. The familiar 'Ding' registered her request. In preparation she slid her butt to the front of her seat, picked up her back pack and sat it on her lap.

Twenty-five minutes on a public bus, although a convenient way to get to and from school, was about all she could tolerate.

The bus jolted to a stop releasing gushes of air from the brakes. After a brief pause the middle exit doors sprung open. Emma stood in line with the other alighting passengers waiting for her turn to exit.

The bus conveniently stopped right at the top of STUYVESANT TOWN leaving only a short stroll to her apartment.

As she stepped from the bus onto First Avenue to commence her short stroll home her senses were awakened by the tantalizing aroma wafting from her favorite Chinese restaurant.

She immediately considered what options she had in her apartment for dinner tonight. She eventually succumbed to

the enticing odors and bought some Chinese takeout on the
way home.

By the time she arrived at her apartment she was salivating
in anticipation of her ready-made dinner. She placed her
keys into a bowl on the kitchen bench and grabbed a bottle
of water from the fridge.

She moved to her lounge room, turned on the TV and sat
back on her couch with her legs crossed, enjoying her
Chinese takeout while catching up on daily events on the
evening news.

With her stomach now full she started to relax as she
reclined back onto her couch. She could quite easily take a
nap right now but she only had about one hour before she
had to get ready for work. So snoozing, despite how
tempting that sounded, was not an option.

Instead, to keep moving and stay awake, she decided to tidy
up after dinner. Her empty Chinese food container and chop
sticks were discarded into the kitchen trash and the empty
water bottle went into her recyclables bin. She looked
around her apartment to check she had everything. THAT
WAS EASY, she shrugged.

On her way to her bedroom she turned off the TV and turned
on her CD player, opting to leave whatever CD was in there
from the last time. The dulcet tones of BRUNO
MARS thumped from her speakers. Emma sang and danced
along as she ran herself a bath. While it filled she went about
laying out her work clothes for tonight.

With the bath full she poured herself a glass of red wine before returning to the stream-filled bathroom. She lowered herself into the soothing hot water, exhaling gently from the tingling sensation of the hot water on her skin.

The thick layer of soft soapy bubbles rose up under her chin as she reclined back into the tub. Emma casually sipped on her wine as she savored one of life's simple pleasures.

It was a little after 6pm by the time Matthew Curry finally arrived at the station and was escorted up to the Homicide squad room. Spence met him in the Bull Pen and relieved the uniform officer of his escort duties.

After shaking hands Spence thanked Matt for coming down on such short notice and told him to take a seat while he spoke to the boss.

Jack was on the phone when Spence leaned in though Jack's office door. Jack held up a finger to Spence then pointed to the chair at his desk. Spence slid into the chair opposite Jack.

Jack hung up the phone a short time later. 'What's up?'

'Matthew Curry's here. Do you want to bring him up to speed?'

'Sure, bring him in.'

Spence returned to Jack's office almost immediately with Matthew in tow. 'You remember Lieutenant Jack Head,' Spence said.

Jack eagerly pushed himself away from his desk, like he was excited to see Matthew – which of course he was. He quickly walked around to Matt's side of the desk with his hand extended to Matt. Matt accepted the gesture with a single shake. Greetings were exchanged.

'You remember the letter you deciphered for us a few weeks ago…' Jack said. Matthew nodded in response. 'Do you think you could do that again?'

Matthew stared blankly back at Jack, then his gaze shifted to Spence. His single eyebrow was raised in an expression of clear confusion. 'What…you want me to decipher the same letter again…?'

Jack looked at Spence then frowned. 'What…No…Look…sit down.' Jack indicated the visitor's chair at his desk.

Matthew calmly lowered himself into the chair and looked up at the standing Jack and Spence.

Jack perched himself on the front of his desk beside Matthew with his arms crossed as he spoke. 'Are you interested in helping us again with some more code breaking?' Jack said.

'Absolutely.' His eagerness overflowed.

'Good. This may take some time. Do you have any plans for tonight?' Jack asked.

'No, no I'm good.'

'Now,' Jack said firmly. He leaned in towards Matthew. 'What you are about to see and hear is part of an ongoing murder investigation. It cannot leave this building. Do you understand?'

'I completely understand,' Matthew said. 'Nothing will be said. You can trust me.'

Jack placed his hand on Matt's shoulder. 'Good to hear....Now do you need to call your Mom to tell her where you are?' Jack asked.

'Yeah, I probably should.'

'OK use that phone out there.' Jack indicated the phone out on Spence's desk. 'Let your Mom know we will drive you home when you are finished.'

Jack shifted his focus to Spence. 'Get him an outside line...' Spence nodded.

With the formalities out of the way Jack and Spence took time to update Matthew on the receipt of the 4th letter and how it appeared to be similar to the letters Matt previously decoded.

Jack told Matt that the literary quote was from a different English author this time: a Samuel Butler. Matt didn't know this author or his novels.

Jack arranged for Spence to get a copy of the letter for Matt and set him up in the first interview room with a lap top.

Jack asked Matthew to keep him updated after he solved each part of the letter.

It took Matthew less than three minutes to answer all the cryptic clues and five minutes to work out the coordinates and enter them into the LATITUDE AND LONGITUDE FINDER website to reveal where the clues directed them to.

Matthew smiled when he poked his head out from the interview room. 'Excuse me, Detective Spencer...'

Spence's head lifted to the voice. 'Yep...' Spence must've noticed the grin. 'Ya done already..?'

Matt nodded. 'The first part...I've worked out the book store...'

Spence pushed himself from his desk and stood. He beckoned towards Matt. 'Come. Let's let the boss know.'

Spence and Matt strolled into Jack's office. Jack looked up from his reading to his entering visitors.

'Matt has solved the first part,' Spence said.

A smile emerged out the side of Jack's face; a rare sight indeed from such a serious man. 'What cha got for me Matt?'

'I've solved the crossword clues and put the numbers into the latitude and longitude finder. The clues are directing you to BARNES AND NOBLE book store at 555 5th Avenue.'

Jack checked his watch. It was just after 8pm. 'If Matt is to break the code tonight, we need THAT book,' Jack said to nobody in particular. He sounded desperate.

'Most stores will be closed for the day by now, Jobs,' Spence said.

'I know... that's what worries me.'

Jack tapped BARNES AND NOBLE into Google on his desktop computer and drummed his fingers on the desk waiting for the results. 'OK, their website says they are open until 9pm on Thursday nights.' Jack again checked his watch. He lifted his desk phone and dialed the book store.

After the call Jack slammed the receiver down and slid open his desk drawer. 'They have a copy of THE WAY OF THE FLESH,' Jack said as he lifted the car keys. 'And they're expecting you...' Jack lobbed the keys to Spence, who caught them with a snatch.

'If you take the FDR and get off at East 42nd Street you can be there in about fifteen to twenty minutes,' Jack said. 'I'll order us some takeout to be delivered while you are gone.'

Emma toweled herself dry after her bath and then stood in front of her mirror examining and even admiring her form. She turned to her left and checked out her flat stomach and profile and then to her right to check out her well-toned butt.

She turned to face away from the mirror and peeped back over her shoulder admiring her fit naked body from the rear. ALL LOOKED GOOD.

Her figure was quite alluring. She had long shapely legs, a tight firm athletic butt and a narrow waist with well-toned abdominals. She had natural voluptuous breasts and a gentle tan.

Her pubic hair was cleanly waxed but that preference was not her own. For reasons unknown to her, many men were excited by females with waxed vaginas.

She wound her long strawberry-blonde hair into a tight bun and then moved into her bedroom to dress into her work clothes, in readiness for her shift.

Her choice of uniform for tonight was a small red leather Bolero jacket. The jacket sat open to expose a black leather push-up bra that intentionally revealed and accentuated her ample cleavage.

She also selected a snug, form fitting red leather mini skirt from her wardrobe and a pair red platform thigh-high boots. She was almost ready.

Next she moved to her dresser and removed a black long haired wig from her mannequin-head wig stand. With a well-practiced move she slipped on the wig and maneuvered it into position.

Instantly she transformed from an attractive strawberry-blonde into a seductive, black haired beauty. She then fitted her red leather Bolero cap onto her silky black hair, clasped on a black leather choker with an array of chains cascading down the front of her chest and she was set.

The baggy sweats and hoodie wearing university student had transformed into her alter ego; a GREENWICH VILLAGE street hooker known by the pseudonym 'NIKKI'. She even amazed herself at how different she looked in the black wig.

Coming from a lower socio-economic family background, raised by a single parent, Emma was not able to rely on her mother to pay for her University tuition. The only way she could study law was to fund it herself.

She quickly realized that waiting on tables, or working in retail stores for minimum wage would not pay for her college tuition, let alone rent or food.

A university friend of hers, who had since graduated, also worked the streets to pay for HER tuition and persuaded Emma to try it as a way to fund her University expenses. Emma tried it and had never looked back.

She did not do drugs and by her choice, she only worked on the busy nights: Thursdays, Fridays and Saturdays, which worked in well for her because her Fridays were free from lectures. About one third of her clients were regulars from her FACEBOOK and *Instagram* pages and the others were 'walk-ups' found during the night.

The tricks of the trade were learned very early on. The more erotic and seductive she was dressed, the more excited the Johns were. The more excited the Johns were, the quicker it was all over.

She intentionally never carried any bills with her so she was not able to give change to the Johns. She also carried extra pairs of panties, most of which she bought for the purpose because some men, particularly her Japanese regulars, asked to buy her panties as souvenirs.

Twenty percent from all her takings was paid to her pimp, LeVander, which increased to 30% on weekends. LeVander was normally a casual guy but he was not averse to hitting females. Rip him off and he would inflict a relentless barrage of physical pain to punish the transgression and breach of trust, as well as to deter recidivism.

He did so comfortable in the knowledge that street hookers do not report assaults from their pimps at the risk of being busted themselves.

Unbeknownst to LeVander, Emma charged much more than the prices he set for his hookers; a very risky practice indeed. But she was gorgeous, clean and incredibly sexy. Most men looking for a hooker gravitated towards her and were happy to pay her prices.

Emma earned between $1000 and $2000 a night from which she was able to adequately cover her University fees, her apartment and still lived very comfortably.

Her biggest fear was not LeVander, whom she believed she could manage. Her fear was being busted for street prostitution and the consequences of such a prior conviction when pursuing a law career.

She often recalled the time she was caught up in a police sweep of street hookers. The arresting copper could see she was not like the others and took a liking to her. When she convinced him she only did it out of necessity to pay for her

University tuition, he was sympathetic and let her go with a warning to be careful in the future.

For reasons unknown to her the same copper now alerts her via text messages when planned raids were occurring in her neighborhood. He asked for nothing in return.

After a short cab ride to her street corner in Greenwich Village she was ready for the long night ahead.

The delivery of Italian take out arrived at the station around the same time Spence returned from Fifth Avenue. Jack and Spence enjoyed a feed of gnocchi pasta, while Matthew devoured a large pepperoni pizza.

Once dinner was out of the way Matthew adjourned to the interview room to decipher the letter with the assistance of the book by SAMUEL BUTLER. Mathew studiously worked through the pages of the book locating the words identified in the code.

In less than five minutes the puzzle was complete. Matthew had deciphered the message in the cryptic killer's 4th letter.

His face struggled to contain the beaming smile as he moved towards Jack's office to tell him the news.

'Are you done already?' Spence asked as Matt approached.

Matthew didn't need to respond. He just beamed a proud smile back at Spence, which was as articulate as any spoken word.

Jack sat at his desk reading when Spence and Matt entered his office. He lifted his eyes to his visitors. He noticed both men had pleased expressions. Jack removed his reading glasses and held them in his hand as he sat back in his chair. His inquiring eyes flicked from Spence to Matt and back. 'What's up?'

Spence grinned. 'He's all done Jobs.'

Jack checked his watch. 'You're kidding...that's fantastic.' Jack gestured to the chair opposite.

Matt slid into the chair. Spence perched himself on the front of the desk.

'Well, what can you tell us...?' Jack said.

Matthew appeared to take great enjoyment in explaining the message he had deciphered. 'As suspected, the message was similar to the 3rd letter,' Matt began. 'Using the coordinates uncovered in the code I was able to establish what the killer's message was...' He lifted his notes and read, 'the next body, a hooker, will be found in MADISON SQUARE PARK with her neck broken. Same deadline of forty-eight hours was provided,' Matt said.

Jack and Spence exchanged a glance. A simultaneous grin emerged on their faces.

'Great job Matt,' Jack said. 'You have no idea how helpful you have been. You might just have saved someone's life...' Jack said.

Matt's smiling eyes shifted from Jack to Spence.

This was Jack's first real breakthrough. He now had a small conduit into the killer's mind. Had the killer's complacency caused him to slip up? The killer would not have expected them to crack the code?

Cautious enthusiasm slowly replaced Jack's excitement. He now knew the location where the body would be dumped. He next had to work out a contingency to try and prevent the murder occurring.

He glanced at his white board, at the three sets of eyes staring directly back at him. This time he confidently held their gaze. This time he was worthy to look them in the eye. He was not going to be responsible for the death of another girl. There was no way he was adding another photo to this collection.

Jack pushed himself from his chair and stood. He rubbed his hands together. 'We gotta get you home Matt,' Jack said as he opened the top drawer and lifted the car keys.

'Want company for the ride back, Jobs?' Spence said.

'Why not,' Jack said.

On the return trip both considered the option of a night cap at Rosie's. But the closer they came to the city, the less interested they became. Instead they called it a night.

Chapter 5

Hudson Street, Greenwich Village was surprisingly busy for 11pm on a Saturday Night, despite the overcast conditions and threatening skies. The one-way street was busy with the constant flow of slow moving cars. Some were passing through, but many were crawling the gutters seeking female company.

The tall leafy evergreens that lined the street, quite picturesque by day, had transformed into black canopies against the moonless night, hovering over the bustling sidewalks. Fluorescent lighting and neon signs from businesses that were still trading, softly illuminated the sidewalks.

For Emma's' alter ego, 'Nikki' this street held a significance different to that of most visitors to the area, particularly between West 10th and Charles Streets. This was where she plied her trade. This was where she sold her services to anyone willing to pay her price.

Her choice of 'uniform' for this popular night of the week was her ever reliable black platform thigh-high boots, buttocks-revealing cut off denim shorts that appeared painted on, a brief red bikini style top that barely covered her nipples and a black leather bolero with matching cap.

From her choice of wardrobe there was no mistaking what she did for a living but there wasn't a guy that passed her who didn't take in a longer than usual glance at her sexy, scantily clad figure.

While standing on the curb she smiled her bright white teeth at the drivers of any slow moving vehicle and any men walking by that showed her interest.

Her Bolero jacket and skimpy top exposed the full shape of her breast, leaving absolutely nothing to the imagination. She was the constant center of attention of male passers-by.

The busier the streets were with tourists to the area, the less approaches by potential Johns she was likely to have. The actions of men approaching one of the street girls appeared to intrigue visitors to the area. Whether they were interested in monitoring the transaction, or disgusted by the action was unclear but their overt gazing intimidated and detered men seeking discretion.

Nikki watched a red colored ford slowly approach. She recalled this was the fourth circuit he had completed along the one-way street. Things were looking promising for her first trick of the night. It had been quiet so far, which was to be expected prior to midnight.

Business always boomed after midnight on a Saturday night once the inhibitions were relaxed and the libidos were fueled from the effects of alcohol over indulgence.

Or there were the more apprehensive tricks who waited until the visitor numbers to the area reduced considerably before approaching a street hooker, to minimize the chances of being seen, or worse, recognized.

She also had to make judgement calls and assess whether the gutter crawlers were undercover cops looking to entrap her. But as she hadn't heard anything from her cop friend, who always alerted her to pending police raids in Greenwich Village, she relaxed slightly. Her razor sharp street instincts had already inferred that this guy was not a cop.

Nikki watched the red vehicle pull over and stop right in front of her. The male driver made eye contact with her, giving off all the signs she recognized. She strutted over to the passenger side door and leaned in through the open window. Her large breast intentionally hung down freely, almost unrestrained and in full view of the driver.

They were her best asset and she made sure she used them to her full advantage. The driver was an average looking European male in his early forties.

'Hi Hun. Looking for some company...?' She offered her standard opening question.

'How much?' the driver nervously blurted back as his eyes flicked between Nikki's eyes and her ample breasts, followed by a quick check along the street in front of him.

Nikki smiled confidently and welcoming. She stared straight back at him and asked, 'what are you looking for Hun?'

It was important to ensure the John asked for what HEwanted. She was mindful that when cops were trying to entrap the girls, they made the girls say what services she offered and her prices.

The driver nervously looked forward, out the front windscreen of his car and then back at Nikki, as though he was searching for the words that were stuck somewhere between his brain and his vocal chords. Although he sat at the wheel of his car, his arousal was obvious to her.

'Head...um...Ah...ho... How much for just head...?' he stuttered nervously in a whispering tone. His head pivoted like a nervous sparrow.

Nikki smiled reassuringly, mindful not to make him feel too self-conscious about his nervousness.

'Two BENJAMINS...'she began, 'and it won't be "just head"...' she said, 'It will be the best head you have ever had, Hon,' she boasted, slightly jiggling her dangling breasts as a teaser.

Head jobs were a service that she performed extremely well, but she had to take great care. She had the misfortune of having two larger than normal eye teeth.

Although relatively indiscernible, she had to be mindful of them when they were so close to a client's sensitive parts. They were quite sharp but she had learned how to keep them out of the way when performing fellatio with a male client.

Despite achieving exactly what she set out to; arouse him by the display of her ample breasts, she still had to suppress the urge to chuckle when she heard him moan with pleasure as he stared lustfully at her jiggling breasts. HOW EASY MEN ARE. A PAIR OF BOUNCY TITS AND THEY'RE HOOKED.

Although she charges $200, as far as LeVander was aware the price charged by his girls for oral sex was $75. Nikki intentionally inflated all her prices because she wasn't working the streets because she enjoyed it. She figured the more profit she could make after LeVander got his 30% cut, the less tricks she had to do. It was purely economics to her.

'OK, get in,' the man said.

'Do you have the two hundred, sweetie...?' Emma said.

The driver reached into his shirt pocket and removed a number of large bills. He quickly peeled off two $100 bills. He folded them in half and handed them to Nikki. She accepted the bills with a pleasing smile. She discreetly placed them down the front of her denim shorts before she opened the car's door and climbed in.

She quickly established he was new to the area, so she directed him to drive to a nearby secluded area down by the Hudson River; an area the girls regularly used for in-car sex.

Experience has taught Nikki to ensure she received payment before disclosing that she insisted all sex acts, including fellatio, were performed with her client wearing a condom. It was a very common requirement in the sex industry, however some of the more skanky girls didn't take these precautions.

The timing of her announcement was everything. By the time she removed the condom from her hand bag, the John's expectations were peaking so she rarely received any resistance. However she was always mindful that some of her work colleagues have been badly beaten for similar requests.

Ten minutes later Nikki was back on her patch. She was still a little perplexed after the driver unexpectedly returned her to where he picked her up. That was not normal. They usually can't get the girl out of their car quick enough once the service is completed.

As the night progressed Nikki continued marketing herself by strolling seductively along her patch with slow deliberate catwalk-model strides. Her tight butt muscles protruded well beneath her cut-off denim shorts. She had removed her jacket and slung it over her shoulder, held onto by a finger. From a distance the shoestring straps on her red bikini-style top gave the appearance she was naked from the waist up.

While casually ambling along her assigned turf she received a text message. It was from one of her FACEBOOK regulars. He was on his way and wanted to arrange a meeting at 'the apartment'.

For Johns that approached her on the street, Nikki's entrepreneurialism had ingeniously pre-arranged the use of a vacant one-room apartment just around the corner. A double mattress on the floor was the only furnishings. On each occasion that she used the room she discreetly slipped the building's Superintendent a twenty on exit. On a good night he could make as much as $200 from her hard work.

Her FACEBOOK regular, a slightly overweight married man in his mid-fifties, was patiently waiting on a bench outside the apartment. In her usual theatrical parading, she sashayed up towards him, overtly flaunting her sexuality to intentionally escalate his libido. She could tell by the look on his face he liked what he saw.

Three hundred and fifty dollars for straight sex and five minutes later she was back on her patch.

LeVander had been monitoring his prize girl. He timed his approach so there was a lull in passers-by. He casually sauntered up beside her with a typical swagger and confidence to seek an update on her last two tricks.

'Wazzup baby girl,' he asked, which was his way of inquiring what her last two tricks were so he could calculate his kick.

'BJ and a straight,' she replied as he mentally worked out his 30% on $225, which in reality, her inflated pricing had earned her double that at $550.

Jack had spent the entire day preparing for tonight's operation aptly named "OPERATION CODE BREAKER". The Homicide Bull Pen over flowed for the pre-shift briefing.

With the approval of the Bureau Chief, two police members from each of the neighboring precincts, as far up as Midtown, had been seconded to his team for the Saturday night operation.

In total there were thirty cops gathered, all eagerly awaiting further instructions. One thing was certain, tonight they all shared a mutual interest in stopping the Cryptic Killer.

Firstly, Jack briefed the group on the background of the killer. This was followed by the deciphered letters and the location where the latest letter disclosed the victim's body would be dumped.

He described the profile of the killer, as provided by the FBI. He also detailed the killer's known MO, and particularly highlighted the fact the killer used a luxury vehicle to pick up his victims.

Based on the killer's pattern and the body dump site, he predicted that either Tribeca, or Greenwich Village would be the killer's next likely target area.

All those in attendance were divided into teams of two and assigned a unit name consistent with their own precinct number.

Confident with his pattern analysis, Jack assigned four teams to the Tribeca and SoHo red-light districts and three teams to the Greenwich Village red-light district.

Using a large map of Lower Manhattan he highlighted the blocks of streets each unit would be responsible to patrol.

The team from 14th Precinct – Call sign UNIT 14 — were assigned a static post monitoring the Waldorf Astoria garage exit onto East 50th Street.

Jack addressed the two man team from Unit fourteen. 'I want you two to position yourselves in East 50th Street, near the intersection with Lexington Avenue.' He indicated the location on the large map. 'The one-way street will direct all vehicles toward you,' Jack said. 'Be aware that we suspect that the Waldorf Astoria Valet Supervisor, Benton Wylie is assisting the killer in acquiring a vehicle. So, ANYluxury vehicle that exits the garage after midnight is to be stopped and checked to confirm the driver is also the vehicle owner. Understood?' Jack said. The Unit fourteen members nodded their understanding.

Jack collectively addressed all the other teams. 'I want you to intercept all luxury vehicles you detect driving in and around your assigned areas, whether the vehicles are passing through, or gutter crawling. If it is a luxury vehicle, stop it. The perp will not own the car he is driving, so full licence and registration details are to be obtained to verify the driver owns the vehicle,' Jack said. 'I don't care if the luxury vehicle has just picked up a hooker, you are to intercept it and verify the driver's details.'

As a contingency plan, in case the killer was able to slip the net he had cast, he posted his own team at discreet vantage points in and around Madison Square Park to monitor the eight entry points into the park.

Jack informed the group that he and Spence would move between all areas coordinating the operation. All units were issued hand held radios set to Channel six. He stressed the normal operational frequency channel was not to be used for this operation.

Jack instructed all units to report in to him when they were in their assigned areas and were to provide regular situation reports to update him.

With a quick check of his watch Jack noted it was 10.30pm. There were no further questions, so the teams were dismissed to allow them time to grab a coffee before departing for their assigned locations.

As the crews vacated the room Jack's eyes met Spence's. His eyebrows raised up in hopeful anticipation as he exhaled long and loud. All was in readiness.

Jack had spent the last two days preparing and checking his operational plan and was confident he had all areas adequately covered, as long as each of the units did their jobs correctly.

The time had ticked past 12.30am and the night air had cooled considerably. There was a distinct feeling of dampness in the atmosphere. Not ideal for Nikki in her scant clothing, suited to much warmer climates.

To stay warm she decided to keep moving up and down her strip. She folded her arms tightly across her chest, hugging her biceps for warmth.

As she arrived at the border to her patch, the intersection with West 10th Street, she walked to the curb to assess what sort of action was around. Passing traffic had reduced to a trickle and pedestrian traffic was meager.

She noticed Lulu, one of her 'street sisters', at the same location, but on the other side of the road. They exchanged a friendly wave when their eyes met.

Emma was about to relocate back towards the other end of her patch, away from Lulu, when she noticed a black car pull in and park parallel to the curb opposite her, near where Lulu stood.

Nikki was unsure if she was interested, or envious, but she paused momentarily to watch. The driver had wound down his window and looked towards Lulu. Nikki nodded as a smile emerged from the side of her face. Lulu was fortunate, given to lack of opportunities from passing vehicles this evening.

About the same time as the black vehicle pulled alongside Lulu's curb, a male customer approached Lulu from the footpath. She hugged the man and they chatted like old friends.

Lulu's interaction with this John distracted her from noticing the black car parked by the curb. After a brief, but friendly discussion, Lulu and her John discreetly moved away from the area, around into West 10th Street and out of sight.

Nikki smiled to herself as she casually commenced her retreat back along her patch of turf, strutting her stuff while her inbuilt radar scanned her surroundings for potential targets.

Folding her arms across her chest in a feeble attempt to generate warmth to her near naked upper body, she started to tire. Her interest and enthusiasm diminished with every step. She checked her phone as she strolled. There were no. messages.

The distinctive shrill of a short, sharp whistle caught her attention. She knew that sound well. It was LeVander's call used to attract the attention of one of his girls. Emma turned towards the direction of the sound.

LeVander stood at the intersection of West 10th Street, about ten yards to the rear of the parked black vehicle. He looked directly at Emma. She turned and walked back towards him, moving onto the roadside. She stopped and held her *what do you want?* hands.

LeVander jabbed a finger at the black car parked where Lulu stood only moments earlier. She understood his succinct sign language. He was ordering her to get her ass across the street and speak to the John in the black car before he drove off.

Emma checked for traffic then trotted across the road towards the black vehicle, a precarious action when wearing six inch spike heeled, thigh-high boots. Her semi restrained breasts bounced freely into themselves as she trotted.

The driver of the stationary vehicle lowered the passenger side window and glanced in her direction, watching her as she approached. She casually pushed out her chest to ensure he noticed her best assets bouncing as she ran.

Nikki slowed to a walk as she neared the car. She adjusted her bikini top then, in her usual manner, she leaned in through the vehicle's open window. Her assets dangled freely.

The unmistakable smell of new leather was first to greet her. It was pleasing to the senses. Her initial recognizance of the vehicle's interior quickly concluded it was an expensive vehicle, presumably owned by someone with money.

She smiled at the driver, pleasantly surprised at what she saw. The driver was much younger than her usual tricks and quite handsome. His closely shaved hair and unshaven after-five shadow produced rugged looks that could see him appear in movies, or grace the covers of glossy magazines. He returned a very pleasant smile back at her.

'Hi handsome. Looking for some company?' she asked.

'As a matter of fact, I am.' He smiled while confidently maintaining eye contact with her. His voice was gentle and quite soothing. For the first time ever she was semi-attracted to one of her clients.

He wore a tailored suit and appeared to be a man of considerable affluence. His choice of motor vehicle clearly supported her assumption. WHY WOULD SOMEONE SO CUTE NEED TO BE PICKING UP STREET GIRLS? But then again, she was not your average street girl.

'What are you looking for Hun...?' she asked.

'Um...' He shifted his gaze out the front of his vehicle, as if thinking for the right words to use, before his focus returned to Nikki. 'I am only seeking oral relief, if that option is possible,' he replied, articulating his preference in a clarity she had not heard before from a trick.

Nikki smiled at him and he returned her smile as he waited for her to respond with her costs.

'I'm a little more expensive than most Hun...but it will be an experience you won't forget - and worth every cent,' she said.

Her comments and over confidence made him smile. He nodded once back at her. His focus shifted to the front of his vehicle. 'And how much is this life-changing experience going to cost me…?' He had a hint of flippancy in his tone. His focus returned to Nikki.

'For someone as handsome you…$300,' She said.

His mouth turned downwards as he slowly nodded. He appeared to be happy with her fees. 'OK. I can do that.'

The driver reached into his jacket pocket and removed his wallet. In an unusual display of trust, he passed his wallet over to her. 'Remove your fee from there,' he said.

Nikki stared momentarily at the wallet held in his extended hand. She slowly reached her hand out to receive the wallet from him, at the same time wondering way he couldn't remove the cash himself and pass it to her. Was this a test of trust?

She accepted the wallet and stood up from leaning on the car and opened it. It was full of bills. She left her hands in full view of the driver while she counted off three, one hundred dollar bills and slipped them out of the wallet. She closed it again and leaned back into the car.

She held up the three spread bills in her hand and passed the wallet back to the driver. The driver smiled as he took back his wallet and returned it to his inner jacket pocket.

'Climb in.' He smiled, extending his hand towards the passenger seat.

Nikki opened the car door and climbed in, still a little puzzled by the wallet thing.

The soft leather seat seemed to envelope her as she eased back into it. It was so comfortable. She sat momentarily with her eyes closed, soaking in the sensation of the welcoming seat. It was a little cool on first touch, but quickly warmed to a comfortable temperature against her body.

The gentle forward acceleration of the vehicle brought her back to reality. She opened her eyes as the driver slowly commenced his journey along Hudson Street. The car just seemed to glide in silence, as if on air.

The interior was sound proofed from any outside engine noises. She smiled to herself, and for the moment she felt like she was part of societies upper echelon as she watched the scenery pass by.

'If it is agreeable with you I have a favorite spot my ex-girlfriend and I use to frequent, down by the East River. It's about a ten minute drive, but I promise I will bring you back when we are finished,' the driver articulated in his now typical eloquent style.

She looked at his reassuring smile and shrugged her shoulders in an agreeing manner. 'Sure. It's your money.' She smiled back at him. 'Can I ask you a question?' She had finally worked up the courage.

'Of course.'

'Why did you hand me your wallet, instead of taking the money out yourself?' she asked.

The driver smiled. 'Maybe I wanted to impress you by showing you I had a lot of cash in my wallet,' he said playfully. Nikki forced out a smile. 'No...I'm just messing with you. But truthfully though...' He held up his left hand. 'I injured the knuckles on my fingers playing basketball and I can't bend them at all. I wouldn't have been able to remove the bills, so...I gave it to you. I trusted you,' he said with a reassuring smile.

Nikki nodded. She accepted his response was plausible. She started to relax a little.

'It's my turn now...' the driver said. 'I have a question for you...'

'O-K,' she said tentatively.

'Do you insist on condoms for oral sex...?' he asked.

The question caught her off guard. She never discussed the use of condoms this early on in a transaction. She was concerned at whether it would cause a change in his personality if she replied in the affirmative.

'As a matter of fact, I do.' Her reply was intentionally confident and direct.

Without removing his eyes from the roadway ahead he smiled and nodded. 'Good to hear,' he said. 'They protect both YOU and ME.'

Nikki smiled back at him, and nodded gently. She started to relax and feel more reassured by his comments. She focused on the illuminated roadway in front and the road markings as they disappeared under their vehicle into the darkness beyond.

Chapter 6

Jack glanced at his watch: It was 3am. He rubbed his forehead. Nothing had been reported from any of the units, not even the Waldorf crew. If his suspicions were correct, the luxury vehicle should have been picked up from the Waldorf by now.

'What was the time the Merc was taken from the Waldorf in the other murders...? It was about two wasn't it?' Jack asked.

Spence thought for a moment. 'Um... yeah it was. The Valet camera was moved just before two...and the car was driven out right on 2am,' he recalled.

Jack lifted his watch to Spence. 'He should've taken a car by now...It's after 3am.'

Spence nodded. 'Unless he is breaking from his previous MO,' Spence said. 'What if that fat prick from the Waldorf...what was his name...Wylie?' Spence said.

'Yep, Wylie...Brenton Wylie,' Jack said.

'Yeah, Wylie...What if he told the perp we had been looking at the garage footage so the perp changed his MO...You know...Different hotel...or different time?'

'He won't change hotels,' Jack said. He was confident. 'Unless he has another Valet in his hip pocket, but he could change his time...' Jack rubbed a thoughtful hand across his chin stubble. 'The only trouble about changing his time to later is, he has less time to clean up everything under the veil of darkness, you know...before the dawn starts to break,' Jack said.

'What about earlier then?'

'Yeah earlier could work, but we've got the Waldorf Crew...Who are they?' Jack asked rhetorically as he looked through his list of resources. He ran his finger down the page, stopping near the bottom. 'Fourteen... We've got Unit fourteen watching the garage and they've been quiet all night.'

Jack drummed his fingers. He was uneasy about how things were, or were not progressing. He instructed Spence to drive over and pay a visit to Unit fourteen.

After a drive of around ten minutes they pulled up behind Unit fourteen's vehicle parked in East 50th Street. Both Detectives from Unit fourteen were still seated in the vehicle.

Jack and Spence alighted from their vehicle and climbed into the back seat of Unit fourteen's car.

'Anyone left the garage since midnight?' Jack asked.

Phil, the older of the two Detectives responded. 'Nope, nothing. It's been a long and boring night so far.'

'So not one car has left the garage since midnight?' Jack clarified.

'No. I just told you...not one car,' Phil repeated with a glance back over his shoulder at Jack.

'What about the Valet, Phil?' Phil's partner said.

Jack and Spence exchanged a glance. 'What about the Valet?' Jack asked.

'Oh yeah... Phil began. 'I forgot. A car came out about 12.20 or so and we jumped on it... but it was only the Valet guy taking a car around to the main entrance on Park Avenue for a guest, so we didn't worry about it.'

'Are you kidding me?' Jack blurted, barely containing his anger. 'I fucking made it clear to you...ANY car leaving the garage was to be stopped and reported to me.'

'But it was just the Valet...we didn't think-'

'That's fucking right...you didn't think... I told you at the briefing that we believed the Valet may be assisting the perp get cars...Fuck Me.' Jack flung the car door open, pushing it out with his foot. He was about alight but paused before doing so. 'Was the Valet driving the car a fat fuck...?' Jack asked before exiting.

'Yeah… he was actually.' Phil was sheepish in his response. He flicked a hand at his colleague. 'We got his details though…what was his name?' He asked his colleague seated beside him.

'Ah…' The other Detective checked his notes. 'Brenton Wylie. Twenty-eight years. Says he's the Valet Supervisor.'

'I fucking know who he is…What type of car was it?'

The younger Detective returned to his note book and read out, 'Um…a black Audi A6…Jersey Plates. We ran the rego and it was registered to the same name the Valet said was staying at the hotel.' The Detective ripped the page from his notes and handed it back to Jack.

Jack snatched the page from the Detective and alighted from the car. He punctuated his frustration by slamming the door forcefully.

Jack and Spence quickly made their way across the road to the Waldorf Security office to review the footage from the fixed camera over the Valet key cupboard from midnight.

The officer shuffled through the footage at an accelerated speed with Jack and Spence hovering over him.

Jack pointed to the monitor. 'Stop… There,' Jack ordered. The camera vision had suddenly moved towards the ceiling. 'What time is that…?' he asked as his focus shifted to the date and time stamp at the bottom of the footage. 'OK…The camera was moved at 12.15am.' Jack looked at Spence. 'You were right…He took it out earlier… and it looks like that prick took it to him.'

Consistent with the other vehicles, this vehicle was also parked in a camera black spot, so there was no footage of anyone approaching the vehicle in the garage.

A review of the garage exit camera however detected a black Audi A6 exiting the garage onto East 50th Street at 12.23am. Although the camera was a distance from the exit, it was unmistakable; the corpulent Wylie was at the wheel. Jack requested, and received copies of the reviewed footage.

From the Security office Jack and Spence made their way around to the Valet station in E50th Street. Jack was furious. His strides were determined and long; so much so, Spence struggled to keep pace with him.

Wylie stood near the hotel entrance when Jack and Spence arrived at the Valet station about three minutes later. Wylie noticed the two men approaching and he smiled at them in a manner typical of a hospitality greeting offered to hotel guests.

The smile on Wylie's face instantly changed to a look of trepidation when he identified that the person striding directly towards him with a frightening look on his face was Lieutenant Head.

Wylie's mouth shortened to a thin straight line. His eyebrows raised and he instinctively took a short step backwards as Jack neared.

Without breaking stride Jack walked straight into Wylie and forcefully rammed his two palms into Wylie's flabby chest, causing Wylie to reel backwards two steps.

'You fucking piece of shit,' Jack blurted. He started to move on Wylie again but Spence interjected.

'Jack...' Spence motioned with his head towards the inside foyer of the hotel.

Jack noticed he was in full view of other hotel staff. He grabbed a generous hand full of Wylie's jacket lapel and physically dragged Wylie over to the more private Valet inlet, where the key cupboard was located. This area had three solid walls and was away from view of the front entrance.

Jack aggressively threw Wylie against the wall. He grabbed him again, this time with two hands.

'You took the car to the killer you fucking prick,' Jack blurted through gritted teeth. He punctuated his comment with a short sharp jab up under Wylie's chin. Jack's frightening eyes were enlarged in pure rage.

'I didn't...I took the car to a guest...I swear,' Wylie pleaded. His eyes too were enlarged, but with pure fear.

'Bullshit...' Jack pulled Wylie forward then slammed him back into the wall. 'Who is the guest?'

'Um...ah...' Wylie stammered. It was uncertain if he was too intimidated to remember, or he couldn't make up a name quick enough under the extreme pressure Jack applied.

'I said who is the fucking guest?' Jack repeated the action of dragging Wylie out from the wall and instantly slamming him forcefully back into it again.

Wylie winced in pain. His eyes closed and his face distorted from the forceful impact against the wall.

Jack heard a command coming from behind him, towards the curb.

'Let him go this instance,' a voice blurted.

One of Wylie's colleagues had observed the physicality being metered out on Wylie and went to alert the Hotel night Duty Manager, who had attended to investigate.

Without releasing his grip on Wylie, Jack glanced over his shoulder at the puny, emaciated looking excuse for a man standing behind him.

Jack shook his head at what he saw. 'We're the police. Fuck off...' he ordered before returning his attention to Wylie.

'Charming...' the Manager said. His arms were folded defiantly across his body.

With Wylie still pinned against the wall Jack repeated his comment. 'I said FUCK-OFF...'

The Manager opened his mouth to speak but paused before closing it again without saying anything, probably erring on the side of caution.

Spence made his way towards the Manager. He removed his badge and held it out for the Manager's inspection. 'We're from New York Homicide. We are investigating a series of murders and this man...' he motioned towards Wylie, 'is under arrest. He is being questioned before we take him down town.'

'Under arrest...?' the Manager questioned, his voice rising with an upward inflection. 'For what...?'

Spence gently grabbed the Manager's stick-like arm. 'You don't need to concern yourself with that right now.' Spence gently guided the man towards the hotel entrance. The Manager tried to resist but Spence reinforced, 'You only have to be aware that he will not be coming back to work tonight,' he said as he continued to steer the Manager away from the scene.

While Spence dealt with the Manager, Jack returned his attention back to Wylie. 'I said who is the fucking guest...?' Jack said. 'I'm not fucking around here.'

'Mr Dawkins...' Wylie blurted. 'He's staying in room 2212.'

With one last aggressive push against Wylie's chest Jack released his grip and pointed to the key cupboard. 'Open it,' he ordered.

Wylie straightened himself up from against the wall and slowly moved over to the key cupboard. His jacket lapels were still frozen in their uplifted twisted distortion from Jack's firm grip.

Once he had the cupboard open Wylie stood to the side. His wide eyes stared at Jack.

'Show me where Dawkin's car keys are?' Jack was not a man to be messed with.

Wylie frowned. 'They're...not there,' he said. 'I told you...he took his car out this morning.'

'What room was he in - 2212 was it?'

'Correct...2212.'

Jack raised his huge fist to Wylie. 'If I go up to room 2212, knock on the door and Mr Dawkins is in his room...I'm coming back down here and I'm going to fuckin' knock you out,' Jack said. 'Do you understand?'

'Yes.' Wylie gulped.

When Spence returned, Jack instructed Spence to wait with Wylie while he began to make his way to room 2212. He had only walked about ten yards before Wylie called out.

'Wait,' Wylie said. Jack stopped and glared at Wylie.

'Don't wake him...' he said slowly shaking his head. 'He didn't leave.' Wylie's head dropped. Jack had called his bluff. 'I took the car around to someone else...Dawkins doesn't know it's gone.' Wylie kept his head lowered.

Jack marched back to Wylie. Without speaking he delivered a leg-weakening forceful open hand slap to Wylie's face. A loud crack ricocheted off the walls of the small Valet inlet.

Wylie slumped to his left. His hand moved to his cheek.

Jack grabbed a handful of Wylie's hair and forcefully jerked his head upwards. Jack gritted his teeth and cocked his fist at Wylie. Wylie held his hands out in front of himself. His terror filled eyes widened.

Spence reached over and gently grabbed Jack's left elbow. 'Not here Jobs,' he said in a controlled but low voice aimed towards Jack's left ear. Jack relaxed his arm and stepped off. His glare remained fixed on Wylie.

In a display of GOOD COP-BAD-COP, Spence stepped in towards Wylie while Jack moved back. 'Right now...you are an accessory to three murders, possibly four if we don't catch this killer tonight...I suggest you start talking, or you better get used to the thought of spending the rest of your life in Rikers.'

'Murders...?' Wylie's wide eyed stare flicked from Spence to Jack. 'I don't know anything about any murders. The guy I gave the car to says he has these dates with hot women he picks up and he wants to impress them by driving a luxury car.' Wylie's tone pleaded with them to believe him.

Spence turned to Jack with a look that expressed he believed Wylie.

Jack moved towards Wylie. 'What's in it for you? He asked.

'He pays me $200 bucks per car. All he has to do is return them before morning,' Wylie said. 'I figure it isn't hurting anyone. The car is just sitting in the garage.'

'It's car theft you idiot.' Jack was aggressive in his response. 'But what's worse, you're giving these cars to a murderer,'

Jack added. 'What's his name...? Who is the guy you give the cars to?' Jack asked.

'I don't know his name... I swear.' Wylie's eyes pleaded.

'You swear...' Jack raised the back of his hand to Wylie. Wylie cowered in fear. 'Just like you swore you gave the car to Dawkins,' Jack said then lowered his hand. He glared at Wylie.

'How do you know this person?' Spence said. Wylie's arms remained raised between him and Jack while his focus shifted to Spence.

'He sends me a text when he needs a car. I find one that is parked out of camera view and he picks it up,' Wylie said.

'But YOU drove it to HIMtonight. Why was that?' Spence asked.

Wylie's head dropped. 'Um... I told him you were here looking at video footage so he suggested that I take it to him in case there were cops around.'

Spence looked at Jack, but Jack didn't return his gaze, instead Jack held his disgusted glare on Wylie.

'If you don't know who he is, how did you first meet him?' Jack asked.

'He came by a few nights in a row, all friendly and chatting. He seemed like a real nice guy. Then he asked me about a business proposition with the cars and I accepted. I only earn minimum wage.'

'Your phone...' Jack clicked his fingers at Wylie then held out his hand. 'Give me your phone...'

Jack snatched Wylie's phone and reviewed the call register. 'It says here you received a call from someone called "BEAR" at 12.05am. Is that him?

'Yes. I only know him as Bear. That's what he introduced himself as. I assumed it was a nickname... Coz he's as big as a bear,' Wylie said.

Jack held the phone out to Spence. 'We've got his phone number,' Jack said.

Jack cuffed Wylie and marched him over to Unit Fourteen's vehicle then placed him into the rear seat. He instructed Phil to arrange for a 'Black and White' to attend and take the suspect back to the station and put him in the interrogation room until Jack was able to return.

Following the latest discovery Jack broadcast a general message to all units. They were now looking for a black Audi A6 with Jersey plates, "BLKAUDI". He also redirected all units away from the red light districts and instructed them to check the river foreshores and all parks in their assigned areas. He expected the perp would have his intended victim by this late stage. Time was running out.

Chapter 7

The handsome driver slowed along First Avenue before turning right into 20th Avenue, heading toward the East River. He looked across at Nikki and smiled. 'We're nearly there,' His smile was reassuring.

Unbeknownst to him, she knew exactly where they were. His choice of location was the riverside directly across from her apartment building. This was HERneighborhood, but it was Emma's not Nikki's. Her apartment building was located in a large estate of twenty-one multi-story apartment buildings beside the river.

Her estate was bordered by First Avenue to the west, East 23rd Street to the north, 20th Avenue to the south, with Avenue C running along the river side of the estate.

The driver crossed Avenue C and continued under the elevated FDR freeway, to a vacant car parking area adjacent to the East River. He parked the vehicle horizontally across two parking bays adjoining a riverside park. Even on an overcast and moonless night the outlook across the river was tranquil.

The man-made sanctuary adjacent to the river was a popular park area for visitors to escape in nature's scenic respite from the otherwise concrete jungle. Picnic areas and lush lawns with ample trees spreading natural awnings over the many outdoor barbecues and picnic tables, all contributed to create the perfect riverside setting.

The area was a popular location during the day, especially at lunchtimes and on weekends but tonight it was deserted. All that could be heard was the wind whistling up the river and the dull hum of the traffic overhead on the freeway.

Under the darkness of night the vibrant green foliage and lawns had assumed dreary shades of gray, while the reflection off the river resembled a mass of molten pewter under the moonlit night sky.

'He we are,' he announced. He looked towards Nikki. She smiled. A moment of awkward silence passed.

'So how do you want to do this?' she asked.

The driver alighted from the vehicle and walked around to the passenger side of the car. She noticed as he passed across the front of the vehicle he was very tall and quite solidly built.

After arriving at her door he opened it and extended a chivalrous hand, a gesture from eras gone by, to help her alight from the car.

'Why don't I sit in YOUR seat,' he said gently assisting her out of the car to her feet. He then sat in the passenger seat, keeping his feet on the ground outside the car. He pointed to the ground between his legs. 'You can kneel down there...It should place you at just the right height,' he added. 'Do you want anything for your knees? He asked.

Nikki lowered herself onto her knees. 'No I'll be OK...Thigh-high boots come in handy sometimes,' she joked.

She reached in to the vehicle and lifted her hand bag from the passenger side foot well and placed it on the ground beside her. Following a brief search of the contents she removed a condom.

When she lifted her focus back to the driver he had already removed his penis through his unzipped fly. He was ready to go. She placed the condom over his erect penis while maintaining seductive eye contact with him as she did so.

Nikki took hold of his penis and began to stroke it as she lifted her eyes back up at him. 'Ready...?'

'Let's do this,' he said with a smile.

Nikki adjusted her position, moving in closer to the vehicle so she could comfortably reach him. When she was in the right position she lowered her head taking him fully in her mouth. Her skillful combination of hand and mouth stimulation caused his penis to swell further in her mouth.

She felt the weight of his hands on the back of her head, guiding her head up and down with her movements. She concentrated on trying to finish him off quickly and didn't notice he had moved one of his hands from the top of her head down to her chin. The hand on her chin exerted considerable pressure, causing her head to tilt sideways slightly. It was uncomfortable and difficult to slide her mouth over his penis.

Nikki winced when he clamped his hands tighter on her head. His hands caused her discomfort. He dragged her head upwards like he was trying to lift her mouth clear of his penis, but she offered resistance, thinking he was close to finishing.

When he jerked her head even harder she stopped sucking to verbally protest at what he was doing. But before she could speak, a sudden sharp and intense pain stabbed up into the base of her skull. For reasons unknown to her, her head was now at right angles and her vision was impaired. Everything was black.

The pressure from his hands on her head suddenly released to the sound of a piercing shriek. Her male client forcefully pushed her head away from his groin.

'You fucking bitch,' he screamed. The once calm and reassuring voice now gurgled with anger. Why was he abusing her? What was so offensive?

It took a few seconds in the confusion of temporary darkness before she realized that her wig had somehow twisted around on her head and covered her face and eyes.

After she replaced the wig, Nikki sat back on her heels. Her John was examining his groin. There was some blood pooling inside the condom. She watched his face grimace in pain as he carefully peeled the condom off to reveal a large angled cut on the shaft of his penis, about one inch below his glans. Blood trickled freely from the cut down into his groin.

Nikki cringed at what she saw. She watched in stunned silence, horrified that she could have done that to a client.

His face distorted and contorted with the pain. He applied pressure to his penis with one hand while he reached into his pocket and removed a neatly folded handkerchief, shook it open and wrapped it around his penis to try and stem the blood flow.

Nikki watched in horror at what she had done. Then it suddenly occurred to her. It wasn't her fault. The sudden jolting of her head to the side while her mouth was still enveloping his penis caused one of her over sized eye teeth to slice though the soft skin on the shaft of his penis, opening up a gaping wound.

But why did he turn her head so sharply? Was this some kind of kinky ritual he followed before ejaculation? Her initial thoughts were a mixture of confusion and sympathy towards her John.

She continued watching with genuine concern as he performed first aid to his groin. Nikki's faced tightened. Her mouth shortened and eyes widened. Suddenly everything fell into perspective. She had an awakening. She realized EXACTLY what had happened. The concern on her face was replaced with alarm.

Nikki knelt upright. Her wide-eyed stare locked onto her client like a deer caught in car headlights. A chill ran down her spine. The hairs on her neck stood upright. He had just tried to kill her, but her mouth hadn't fully cleared his penis when he jolted her neck. Having his penis in her mouth actually saved her life.

'Fuck,' she shouted as she sprung backwards up to her feet. The John lunged at her with his free hand and tried to grab her but Nikki arched her hips back and shuffled out of his reach.

Adrenaline now coursed through her veins. He started to adjust himself in the seat to pursue her. Before he could move, she forcefully kicked at him, firmly jabbing the six inch heel of her boot into his chest. The driver grunted as he collapsed back into the vehicle, his freehand now pressing on his chest.

Her fear now escalated along with her heart rate. Her fight or flight instincts told her to run. But could she out run him in these boots? Where would she be safe? She fled towards the rear of the car, stopping suddenly . MY HANDBAG. IT'S GOT MY ID; MY ADDRESS; MY APARTMENT KEYS – SHIT.

She turned and ran back to the open door and scooped up her hand bag in one motion before turning and fleeing. The driver sat with his head bowed examining his wound.

He screamed to the fleeing Nikki, 'Yeah, you better run bitch...you're fucking dead when I catch you.'

Her instincts led her across Avenue C towards the grounds of her apartment building. She didn't want to look back to see if he was pursuing her. She just put her head down and ran. Her spike heels and thigh-high boots restricted her normal fluent loping running style into short careful steps.

Her heart raced. Her mouth was dry. She could hear the heavy plodding of his large feet behind her. His large strides were closing in on her with every step. Her heart pounded in her chest. The pit of her stomach was heavy. She knew he would tackle to the ground at any stage. Her legs were weak from fear. She could hear him breathing heavily as he pursued her. He must be close, but she willed herself to keep pushing forward.

Nikki sprinted through the gate of her estate and ran straight up the sealed path and into the gardens where the depths of the darkness wrapped around her and swallowed her up from view.

In the temporary sanctuary of the shadows from the estate's many trees she stopped to look back behind her. She frowned. There was no-one there. WHERE THE HELL DID HE GO? Her darting eyes scanned the darkness. Her heart battered against her ribs and the blood in her ears pounded as she stood, hands on knees, mouth wide open sucking whatever air she could into her aching lungs.

DID HE DOUBLE AROUND TO THE FRONT TO AMBUSH ME? Her head scanned the grounds. Her eyes squinted into the darkness, listening to any sound foreign to the gardens.

The grounds of her estate consisted of several apartment buildings towering over a forest of majestic trees throughout, with manicured lawns bordered by meticulously maintained garden beds that flank sealed pathways. Six-foot high square shaped tree hedges softened the base of each building and provided privacy screening for the building entrances.

Nikki was now back in Emma's world. She couldn't see him. She quickly moved off the sealed pathway and onto the lawn. The damp ground squelched as it swallowed the heels of her boots with each step.

She sought refuge behind a lush hedge adjacent to her building. The ground on her bare skin was cold as she sat down under the blanket of darkness to gather her thoughts.

The blood in her ears continued to pound. Her pulse raced. She felt sick in her stomach. Her eyes darted through the darkness. WHERE IS HE?

From her vantage point she listened for footsteps, or any discerning sounds that suggested the presence of her attacker. There was nothing. As she calmed she realized he wasn't closely pursuing her. She must've imagined it in her fleeing terror.

After a brief pause she peered through a small aperture in the foliage, towards the estate gateway. She held her breath to control the sound of her labored breathing. There was no sign of him. She squinted into the darkness as she carefully scanned the gardens looking for her hunter.

The picturesque gardens with their abundant green tones had transformed to dreary shades of gray under the darkened skies. The prevailing shadows now provided multitudes of darkened hiding places scattered throughout the estate.

HAD HE MOVED TO ONE OF THOSE BLACK VOIDS WAITING TO POUNCE? WHERE THE FUCK IS HE?

The Adrenalin that coursed through her veins caused her to tremor. Her darting eyes scanned her surrounds. WOULD HE SUDDENLY STRIKE UNEXPECTEDLY?

Despite the cool temperatures, beads of perspiration formed on her forehead. Tears rolled freely down her cheeks as she panted uncontrollably.

If she ran to her building she could risk leading him straight to her apartment. But she had to do something. If she remained where she was it would only be a matter of time before his systematic search of the grounds located her cowering behind the hedge.

She remembered her mobile phone. She could call the police. But what would she tell them? She was an illegal street hooker. She rationalized her predicament. 'Shit' she blurted under her breath.

She listened a little longer in the silence for any discernible sounds. There was nothing. She slowly peered around the hedge. She squinted back towards the gateway and across the road. His car was still parked in the parking lot. She strained her eyes further. The car's interior light was on, but the car appeared to be empty. WHERE IS HE? She quickly scanned the grounds. Her focus returned to the car. Her heart rate started to climb causing her temples to throb.

THERE. In the darkness she saw him round the rear of the vehicle. He walked towards her grounds. She froze. Her muscles locked with terror. He was coming for her but at least she could now see him.

Her survival instincts kicked in. She still had time. While continuing to monitor him as he approached, she unzipped both her boots and removed them, followed by her hat. She had to guide him away from her apartment building. Fortunately for her, he had no idea she would know this area so well.

Keeping low and close to the building, moving under the veil of darkness, she moved to a nearby fork in the pathway. To the right the path snaked further into the estate and towards her building. To the left the path eventually made its way out of the estate onto 20th Avenue.

After a quick check of her pursuer's progress, she kept low as she ran up the left fork and dropped her first thigh-high boot onto the path, just past the fork. She then quickly moved forward five or six yards and dropped the second boot so it lay conspicuously across the path. Moving a further three yards on she placed her upturned leather bolero hat on the grass, immediately beside the path. She kept her black wig on to help conceal her fair hair against the dark voids in which she cowered.

She moved from hedge to hedge with ninja-like stealth, as she skulked her way to a position where she could monitor both the estate gate and the fork in the path. She checked his progress once again.

She inhaled when she noticed his large silhouetted frame standing motionless at the Estate gate. She squeezed her nose and lips to suppress a scream when she saw him so close. He now hunted her.

She watched as he slowly and methodically walked up the path. His head turned left to right. He was listening for any sounds that would disclose her location.

As he approached her position she held her breath and froze, watching him through the hedge foliage. Her eyes flared when she noticed he now wore latex gloves. She watched as he reached the fork in the path and stopped. He slowly pirouetted around as his eyes scanned the grounds for movement or evidence of her. He was now only yards away from her flimsy leafy shelter.

She inhaled quickly as he started to walk along the right fork directly towards where she cowered. Her ploy had failed. She bit down on her lip and held her breath. The blood thumping in her ears was deafening. Her chest felt like it would explode. Should she make a run for it? She was fit and could probably out run him? But her legs felt like jelly. She felt weak and sick with fear. The salty bitterness of bile filled her mouth as she fought back the urge to vomit.

He suddenly stopped walking and turned. He looked back in the direction from which he had just walked. He turned and quickly walked directly towards the thigh-high boot she strategically placed on the path.

He lifted the first of her planted boots and examined it briefly before scanning the immediate area. He then noticed the second of her boots and moved towards it and picked it up. His gaze was now ahead of him along the path.

He continued to move away from her in the direction her ruse had intended. He veered across the path and scooped up her hat without breaking stride. She watched as he walked along the path and into the darkness and out of her view.

Emma exhaled slowly, trying to keep her breathing under control. She waited and watched, frozen to her position behind the hedge. He would come back soon. He had to, his car was in the car park across the road.

She had no idea how long she had been crouching behind he hedge. One minute felt like an eternity. Her sparse clothing provided little resistance to the icy morning temperatures and the unforgiving ground sucked what little heat she had left from her body.

She was freezing. She could feel the muscles in her arms and legs start to stiffen. She could try running to her apartment building, but she would have to cross the path and risk detection.

In what seemed like an extended period of time, but in reality was only minutes, her attacker emerged from the darkness, walking back towards her along the left path. He carried her boots and cap.

At the fork in the pathway he stopped and stared in her direction, as if a sound alerted him. She froze, holding her breath, wondering if her light skin tone contrasted against the darkness around her. After a brief pause he looked at his watch then continued down the path and out the exit gate onto Avenue C.

Nikki sat in silence as she watched him walk out the gate and across the road towards his vehicle. Her hand covered her mouth. A short time later the car's revving engine started up. She saw the car's headlights illuminate before the vehicle executed a U-turn and drove to her right and momentarily out of sight.

She quickly jumped from her hiding place and ran towards the Estate's gate, keeping under the shadows of darkness. Her bare feet squelched in the damp lawns as her unimpeded strides were now long and flowing.

When she arrived at the outer gate she hugged herself close to the tall boundary hedge and slowly peered around to her right, into Avenue C. His vehicle exited the river side parking lot 100 yards along, before proceeding west into 20th Avenue.

In the still of the night she could hear the acceleration of the engine and eventually, it faded in the distance. He was gone.

Emma cupped her face in her hands as she burst into tears. Her hands trembled and her legs shook. She suddenly jerked to her side and vomited onto the garden bed beside her. She stood crouched over with her hands on her knees, spitting and coughing as she experienced three more violent surges before it would pass.

Emma inhaled deeply to control her emotions as she made her way up to her apartment. Once inside she quickly secured the door behind her. Despite being comforted in the knowledge that she watched him driving away down 20th Avenue, she still paused to look through the door's peephole, just to make sure she wasn't followed.

She poured herself a shaky glass of wine and sat on her sofa, hugging her knees tightly up to her chest while she reflected on what had just occurred. The reality of what happened was starting to resonate. He had just tried to kill her. Her stomach churned at the thought. Her hand shook as she took a sip.

What should she do? Her pondering eyes darted. She decided to call the police. She jumped up and grabbed her telephone handset and returned to her sofa. Her shaky finger pressed 9-1, then she paused with her finger hovering over the number one button. But what would she tell the police?

Would they be sympathetic? She hit the "End Call" button to disconnect the line.

For the next few seconds Emma gently tapped the phone on her chin, staring blankly while she considered her options. She then turned the phone display to towards her and again dialed 9-1. Her finger again hovered over the number one button, while she reasoned with her conscious mind.

WAIT...I WOULD HAVE TO EXPLAIN TO THE POLICE I AM A STREET HOOKER. HOW WOULD THAT AFFECT MY LAW CAREER? WHAT IF THE TV AND NEWSPAPERS BECOME INVOLVED? The parallel lives she worked so hard to keep apart would suddenly collide. She would be exposed. What would her mom think about her nocturnal activities?

She then started to justify to herself why it wasn't necessary to call the police. All the justifications raced through her mind. HE DIDN'T PHYSICALLY HURT ME. HE SCARED THE SHIT OUT OF ME, BUT HE DIDN'T HURT ME. I AM SAFE NOW. HE IS GONE. HE DOESN'T KNOW WHERE I LIVE. HE'S THE ONE THAT WAS HURT, NOT ME.

Emma brushed her fringe from her eyes with the back of her hand as she stared at the phone in her hand. She wanted to call the police but the unknown consequences were too much for her to risk. She pressed the "End Call" button on the phone to disconnect the line. She gently lobbed the phone onto the sofa beside her. She reached for her glass and emptied it in one quick motion before re-filling it and repeating the action.

The over sized railroad station clock, which hung as a prominent feature on her lounge wall, showed it was 2.20am. She started to feel dirty. The thought of her John made her skin crawl and she shuddered. She needed a hot shower to warm up and to cleanse herself of him.

Chapter 8

With the exception of the occasional static crackling over the airwaves, the operation's radio channel remained silent. Jack started to concede that with every minute that passed, the chances of another victim before the night was out increased exponentially.

Jack couldn't help but rue the missed opportunity. If the team from the 14th did their job, the perp would have been caught by now. Instead, he was still out there.

As the darkness started to give way to the new day, Jack still had an ace up his sleeve. The killer didn't know they had cracked the code and would be waiting for him if he tried to dump his latest victim. While it won't save the girl, the perp won't get away with it. Jack checked the time: 5am

'It should've been back by now,' Jack said thinking out loud. 'And Fourteen haven't called to advise...unless they missed it. If the car hadn't returned, maybe he was still out there and hadn't killed his victim yet.'

'Maybe he needs the fat fuck to help him return the car...Maybe the perp couldn't find Wylie so he panicked and dumped it,' Spence said.

Jack nodded. 'But he would have to drive by the garage to look for Wylie and Unit Fourteen would've...SHOULD'VE jumped on him,' Jack said.

'You've got Wylie's phone. There haven't been any calls...?' Jack said, as a question.

Spence checked Wylie's mobile phone. 'Nope.' He shook his head. 'No calls ORtext messages.' He returned the phone to his jacket pocket.

Jack flicked the back of his hand towards the front of the vehicle, 'Let's go to the Waldorf.'

Following a high speed five minute drive Spence pulled in behind Unit fourteen's vehicle. The team were maintaining their vigil over the garage. Jack sent Spence in to review the CCTV footage of the garage entrance, while he went to talk to the Detectives.

Phil looked as though he had just woken up as he wound down his window to Jack. 'Long night...?' Jack said as he squatted down on his haunches by the open window.

'You've got no idea,' Phil said.

'The black Audi hasn't returned...?'

'There hasn't been ONE car return to this garage since midnight,' Phil moaned.

Jack remained in his squatting position as he cast a curious eye east and west along East 50th Street while he considered his options.

'OK, Thanks.' He tapped the window sill twice as he stood up. He crossed the street on his way to the hotel security room to meet Spence.

The guard buzzed Jack into the restricted CCTV viewing room. Spence watched on as the guard fast forwarded the footage on the main monitor.

'Nothing so far,' Spence updated.

'That's it,' the security guard said. 'We're now up to current time.'

Spence caught Jack's eye and jabbed his head towards the door. Jack nodded.

Spence tapped the guard on the shoulder as a sign of gratitude, 'Much appreciated,' Spence said and they left the room.

Once clear of the Security room Spence said, 'The vehicle never returned. I think we should drive around the area...The chances are he's dumped the car nearby.'

'Doesn't make sense...What about the body?' Jack said. 'He doesn't return the car until he has dumped the body.'

'We don't know that he hasn't, Jobs.'

Jack lifted his portable radio and contacted his units positioned at MADISON SQUARE PARK for an update. The response he received quickly reassured him that no vehicle had entered the park from any direction, and in no way was a body dumped on their watch.

Jack shrugged. Nothing seemed to make sense. 'OK, let's go for a drive,' He motioned in a circling action indicating the immediate vicinity of the Waldorf.

Spence drove east along East 50th Street, turned right in Lexington Avenue and right again into East 49th Street. As expected, the streets were deserted as most of the general population would be experiencing REM sleep at this time before rising to face the challenges of the new day.

While slowly cruising up E49th Spence pointed up ahead towards the sole vehicle parked about two-thirds along the street. It was a black Audi A6, parked parallel to the left curb.

Jack checked the details he was earlier handed by Unit Fourteen. 'That's it,' he said. Jack scanned the street. 'Something's not right...none of this fits the profile, or MO.'

Spence pulled up behind the vehicle. His car's high-beam illuminated the abandoned vehicle. With guns drawn both men alighted from their police vehicle and cautiously approached the Audi.

Jack's eyes were fixed solely on the Audi's interior, in case someone was armed and lying down in the car. Spence scanned around the immediate area in case of a planned ambush.

As a team they knew one another better than any married couple, and each knew their respective role to ensure the other's safety.

Jack inched along the side of the car, peering cautiously inside. As he reached the driver's door he lifted his eyes to Spence and shook his head. 'Empty,' he said. Both men quickly scanned the immediate area looking for movement, or anything that was out of place; there was nothing.

Jack returned his torch light to the vehicle's interior. There was no property, or anything appearing out place. He was mindful of the effectiveness of imported vehicle's alarm systems so he gently tried the door handles. The vehicle was secured. He briefly rested the back of his hand on the vehicle's bonnet. He then moved to the vehicle's front grill and held his hand in front of it.

'It's been here a while,' Jack said. 'This doesn't fit Spence. Why is the car dumped out here and not returned to the garage...? And if he dumped the car...where did he dump the body?'

'IS there a body?' Spence said.

'Well, his letter mentioned there would be a body tonight...And based on the three previous letters...' Jack said, 'we have to treat the threat as genuine.'

Spence walked around the Audi. His torch light searched under the car for any incriminating evidence that may have been inadvertently dropped. He stopped at the rear passenger side wheel. 'Jack,' he called as he reached into his pocket and removed a single latex glove.

'What ya got?' Jack made his way over to Spence.

Spence indicated the rear wheel while he positioned the glove loosely in his palm. He reached under the rear wheel arch and removed a set of car keys that were perched on top of the tire. Spence stood back upright and held out the keys enveloped in the latex glove. 'They've obviously been left for someone to pick up the car later,' Spence said.

'And Wylie couldn't pick it up because he's in custody,' Jack said.

Jack retrieved a plastic bag from their vehicle to seal the keys in the bag for examination at a later stage. He then arranged for a Forensic Crime Scene unit to attend and examine the vehicle and scene for any evidence.

'At the moment this is only the recovery of a stolen vehicle,' Jack began. 'We have no information or evidence to suggest it WASused in a murder tonight.'

Had Jack been outsmarted once again by this perp? Was this 4th letter a cunning diversion? Could the perp possibly have known they had finally cracked his code? Had the perp read him like the proverbial book and while Jack had strategically deployed resources elsewhere, the perp was able to quietly pounce on his 4th unsuspecting victim?

A "black and white" with two officers was assigned to crime scene protection until the Forensic team arrived.

Once clear of the scene Jack and Spence returned to the station to speak to Wylie.

During the drive back to the station Jack checked the time. It was 5.33am. 'Either we have the profile completely wrong and he has dumped the body somewhere else, which doesn't make sense, or the letter was a smoke and mirrors cover up and he's duped us,' Jack said.

'Or...he didn't go through with it for some reason,' Spence said. 'Maybe all the cops in the red-light areas served its purpose...you know...spooked the perp...stopped him picking one up.'

Jack shook his head. 'I don't know...maybe. I'd like to think so. But something just doesn't seem right.'

Jack's gut had never let him down in thirty years of policing. He'd learned to trust his instincts and tonight, something just didn't seem right. The change in MO suggested that something went wrong. The perp changed his mind, or maybe he was interrupted...or he just never went through with it. Maybe he had fallen ill, or was in an accident. Maybe he was arrested for something unrelated before he could commit the murder. Maybe....maybe...maybe. Jack stopped himself.

Jack thoughts sounded desperate and desperation was a sign of weakness in the world of Lieutenant Jack Head. He had done all he could. He had prepared well and deployed effectively. All he could do now was wait and see if a body was discovered somewhere in the morning light. He would then have to deal with any changes in MO from there.

'NOOOO!' Emma screamed as she sat bolt upright. Her muscles tensed. Perspiration ran into her eyes. She panted heavily like she had just completed a 100 yard sprint. Her chest heaved to drag in what oxygen it could. Her eyes were wide open in fear, as she slowly scanned her environment while her conscious brain limped awake from its slumber.

'Shit,' she said, rolling her eyes. She collapsed back onto her sofa in the realization she'd just had a nightmare. She draped her arm across her forehead and lay there staring at the ceiling while she tried to calm the rapid rhythmic pulsing in her chest, temple and ears.

The therapeutic benefits of her hot shower had served its purpose. The hot water had sufficiently relaxed her enough to allow her to doze off on her sofa for a couple of beneficial hours sleep. That was until the visions of her attacker chasing her through the streets invaded her restful slumber.

She glanced across at her large wall clock. The hands on the large roman numerals pointed to 5.50am. She remained for two or three more minutes, still deciding what she should do.

Should she let it go and just move on? What if he did this to someone else? But that's not her problem...is it? What if..., she suddenly stopped herself and sat bolt upright. Her wide eyed stare was fixed straight ahead in contemplation. What if he came back looking for her? He knew where her patch was in Greenwich Village. LeVander couldn't protect her all the time. 'Shit,' she said as her eyes darted.

Her eyes fell to the telephone handset on the floor beside her. She gazed at it for several contemplative seconds. *If I don't do this, I will never be able to relax. I will just have to manage the fall out if and when it happens.*

She picked up the handset and promptly dialed 9-1-1. Her mind was made up to call... *Wait...* Or was it?

Two or three seconds of silence followed before the chirping ring tone pulsed in her ear. After the second ring her questioning fears once again took control and she promptly disconnected the call.

She stared at the phone in her hand, completely lost in her own confusion. *What should I do?*

Emma startled when her phone started ringing in her hand. She glanced at the phone's display. There was no number displayed. Her heart rate rocketed. She cautiously answered the call.

'Yes.' She was curt, hoping the caller would feel the strength and confidence in her voice, in case it was her attacker.

'Hello... ma'am. This is 9-1-1 dispatch, we just received a hang up call from this number. Is everything alright ma'am? Are you OK?'

Emma didn't answer. She was too busy biting down on her lip to suppress her emotions.

'Are you in any danger ma'am?' The concerned female voice on the other end inquired.

Emma took a breath. 'I'm OK,' she said 'I...I... just changed my mind.'

'What is your emergency? Can we still help?'

'No...I'm good,' she said. Her tone sounding more abrupt that appreciative.

'Ma'am don't answer me straight away, Just listen to my voice... Is someone there preventing you from talking to me?' the operator asked.

'No...no it's not...I...I...' Emma's words trailed off as a wave of emotion engulfed her. She broke down in tears, sobbing uncontrollably. Her body heaved in spasms with each sob.

The compassion and concern coming from the anonymous voice on the phone broke down the flimsy defensive wall she had slowly been erecting over the past three hours.

'Ma'am are you alright...? Do you need the police...? Ma'am...? Ma'am?' The concern in the operator's voice grew louder. 'Ma'am... ARE YOU ALRIGHT?' The voice rose to a yell.

Emma positioned the phone back to her ear, exhaled loudly and informed the operator that someone had tried to kill her earlier tonight. She was safe now, but didn't know what to do.

The 9-1-1 operator remained on the phone talking to Emma, calming her to ensure she was safe, safe from intruders and safe from herself as the operator skillfully elicited the circumstances of the night's events.

Emma told the voice on the phone everything. She was someone Emma had never met but that didn't stop her revealing all that had happened to her tonight. It was like she subconsciously tried to purge all her fears to the sympathetic ear on the other end of her phone.

Chapter 9

Jack and Spence stared through the two-way mirror at Wylie seated in the interrogation room. 'I wonder how much this prick knows...' Jack said, thinking out loud. 'OK...let's get it done.'

Jack moved to the viewing room exit door. At the door he stopped and pointed to the video camera. 'Turn that thing off,' he said before exiting. Spence grinned as he complied.

Wylie jumped like a frightened rabbit as Jack and Spence burst through the door. His head snapped towards them as they entered. His frightened eyes were wide with concern.

'Am I going to be here much longer...? I've been here for hours.'

Jack slammed his folder on to the table. A deafening crack sound bounced off the walls of the small room.

Jack struck Wylie with an open hand to the back of his head. Wylie's shoulders lifted and his head turtled down into his body. His eyes were shut as he cringed in pain while his hands grabbed the point of impact.

Before Wylie could open his eyes, Jack lifted his foot and forcefully pushed Wylie's upper body away from him. Wylie desperately grabbed at the back of his chair as he started to fall but that only served to drag the chair down to the floor with him. His substantial frame hit the floor with a muffled thud.

Wylie cowered on the ground in fear. Jack glared down as he jabbed a finger at Wylie. 'You don't have the fuckin' right talk to me until you are asked a question,' he said through gritted teeth. Jack's eyes thinned. 'And you will leave when Itell you to leave...Got it...?'

'Yes,' Wylie whimpered, as he started to get up from the floor.

Jack used his foot to push Wylie back down. Wylie's body collapsed from the force. 'I didn't say you could get up,' he said firmly. 'You are where you belong, you piece of shit. Now...' Jack jabbed an aggressive finger at Wylie. 'We are going to ask you some questions...One bullshit answer...Just one,' he said punctuating his comment with a clenched fist. 'The world of pain I will unleash on you will make you regret the day you were born...' He glared at Wylie cowering on the floor.

Everyone receiving the Jack Head stare-down instantly knew this guy meant business. You instantly know that you don't mess with him when he was in this mood; big, strong, angry and incredibly intimidating.

'Right now you are an accessory to three murders and you want to fucking hope like hell it's not four.'

Wylie opened his mouth to speak, but quickly closed it again when Jack glared at him. Jack waved the back of his hand at Wylie. 'Get up,' Jack ordered.

Wylie re-positioned himself at the table. His submissive eyes flicked between Jack and Spence. His puppy dog eyes welled with tears. Jack had broken him. Wylie would now be fully compliant.

Wylie portrayed as a cocky, educated know-it-all clean skin, who had never been in trouble with the law before. In his own mind he knew everything about the law. He knew his rights but his naivety had no idea how things worked in the real world. Rights don't mean shit in the inner sanctums of a police station with cops like Jack Head towering over you behind closed doors.

Wylie's perfect world had never experienced THIS side of policing before. It was the side that the public didn't usually see in this contemporary era of political correctness. This side of Jack and cops like him, was usually reserved for hardened criminals. Wylie was scared and that was exactly what Jack had intended.

Jack perched himself on the table beside Wylie. His arms were folded to intimidate as much as he could. 'What was the arrangement when you drove the car out of the garage this morning?'

'Um...I took it around to East 49th Street and parked it. I put the keys on the passenger side rear wheel for Bear to pick up,' Wylie said.

'He wasn't there?' Jack asked.

'No… I didn't see him.'

'What was the arrangement for the return of the vehicle?'

'He had to return it by 4 or 4.30am to make sure it was back in the garage…in case the owner was an early riser and needed it.'

'We found it parked in East 49th Street. The keys were how you left them. Are you saying that wasn't the arrangement for the return?'

'No… He was to contact me when he was ready to bring it back. Once I returned it to the garage I would move the camera while I return the keys to the cupboard.'

'How did you get paid if he wasn't at the drop off?'

'He came by yesterday and paid me…He usually pays me the day before… It was easier that way.'

Jack glanced over his shoulder at Spence, seated on the other side of the table behind him.

Jack's mind raced. MAYBE THE CAR WAS NEVER PICKED UP IN THE FIRST PLACE. MAYBE IT HAD REMAINED WHERE WYLIE HAD INITIALLY PARKED IT, UNTIL THEY DISCOVERED IT LATER.

'Exactly WHERE in East 49th Street did you park the Audi?' Spence asked.

'About half way down the street in a parking bay on the left hand side.'

Jack's eyebrows arched. *That was a different position to where they located it.* 'Half way down...not two-thirds of the way down?' Jack clarified.

'No definitely half way. I parked it opposite the Waldorf's gold doors...you know the two gold colored doors opposite the lane that runs down to the Intercontinental.'

Jack glanced at Spence. 'We found it further up the road...so it's been used then,' Jack said. 'Why did he dump it instead of returning it as planned?'

'I honestly have no idea. I've been sitting here all morning.' Wylie's focus snapped to Jack. His face tightened and his shoulders tensed as he monitored Jack's reaction to his comments.

Jack allowed the comment to slip by. He was distracted while his mind ran through the likely reasons why the car was dumped.

Spence gestured to Jack and they moved away from Wylie and huddled near the door. Spence whispered to Jack. 'Maybe the perp saw Unit Fourteen parked in East 50th and decided to abandon it,' Spence said.

Jack nodded. 'Makes sense.'

Jack returned to Wylie. Spence remained leaning against the door. 'What can you tell me about "Bear"?' Jack asked.

'Not much really.'

'How many times have you met him?'

Wylie shrugged. 'Five or six.'

'Where did you meet him?'

'At the hotel.'

'Each time?'

'Yes sir.'

'How old is he?'

'I didn't ask him.'

'Guess,' Jack blurted.

Wylie's shoulders instantly rose up and his head withdrew.

'Ah... um...I'd say about....twenty-five...twenty-six,' he said cowering away with his arms lifted in defense.

'Did he say where he lives... where he is from?'

'Never discussed it.'

'Describe "Bear" to me'

'Um... solid... about six feet...eight or nine...blue eyes... really blue. Um...'

'Solid-fat, or solid-muscular?' Jack clarified.

'No... muscular...really strong looking.'

'Caucasian.'

'Yes.'

'Facial hair...?

'No, clean shaven and he had really closely shaved hair. Not receding, shaved.'

'Did you notice any scars or tattoos on him...? On his hands, neck, arms...?'

'None that I could see.'

'Does Bear discuss his "dates" with you at any time...? Who the girls are...where he knows them from...?'

'No, and I don't ask. He just says he has a hot date...I don't ask too many questions. He just pays me and that's all I'm worried about.'

Jack glanced at Spence. 'Do you have anything to add...?' Jack said. Spence returned a very slight, almost indiscernible nod to Jack.

'OK. I'm going to send someone in here shortly and you are going to give them an accurate photo-fit description of Bear. Are we clear?' he said staring Wylie down.

'Yes Sir.'

Jack's mobile phone began to ring. He quickly answered the call. 'Jack Head. Sure, give me a minute,' he said then signaled to Spence before both men exited the interrogation room.

With the phone held low Jack instructed Spence to contact the TELCO and obtain the owner details for the phone number that Wylie had in his phone under the contact for "Bear".

Jack returned the phone to his ear. 'Back again. Go ahead.' Jack wedged his phone between his shoulder and ear. He slipped his pen from his shirt pocket, opened his folder and quickly started to scribble.

'Aha... how long ago...? Aha...' he frantically scribbled down notes. 'Peter Cooper Village...I know it...yep...was she injured...? Aha...how old is she...? Aha...Can she describe him...? Great...OK...He what...? On his —', Jack cut himself short. His face cringed. 'I can be there in ten...' Jack hung up his phone and returned it to his pocket.

After arranging for an officer to compile a photo-fit ID from Wylie, Jack met Spence in the corridor and they made their way to the garage.

'Where we going...?' Spence asked as he moved to keep pace with Jack.

'Just got a call from 9-1-1 dispatch. Looks like we have a lucky one that got away from our killer earlier tonight. Peter Cooper Village,' he said.

'That's great. This'll be interesting,' Spence said. 'She should be able to give us a first-hand insight into who our perp is and his MO.'

Spence then updated his inquiries from the TELCO. 'No luck on the number...it's a burn phone– as we expected,' Spence said.

Jack shrugged it off. He was more focused on this latest victim — the one that got away.

'That explains it...' Jack blurted. 'He fucked up...That's why there hasn't been a body and why he dumped the car....' The pieces of the puzzle from the night's events started to fall into place. 'You wanna hear something funny...?' Jack said, unable to contain an unsympathetic wry grin. 'This girl we are going to see, this hooker, bit the killer on the cock when she was giving him head...sliced it open like a ripe melon apparently...that's how she was able to escape from him.'

'Urrgh,' Spence moaned. His face distorted.

'Yeah, and apparently the injury was quite bad.' Jack stopped in his tracks.

'What's up?' Spence asked, stopping beside Jack. Concerns lines formed on his face..

Jack removed his phone and dialed. He instructed the person on the other end to arrange a check of the ERs from every hospital and medical center in the greater NYC area to see if any male was admitted with an injury to his 'Johnson.' He smiled to himself as he disconnected his call. 'Karma's a bitch ain't it,' he smirked.

Chapter 10

Emma peeked through the small security peep hole in her apartment door after responding to a firm knock. 'Police...' was the firm reply.

'I'm sorry gentlemen...can you hold up your badges so I can see them please.'

Both men complied and then waited for a brief moment. The tell-tale clicking of door locks announced they had passed her initial security screening and were about to be granted entry.

Aware they were traveling to interview a street hooker who had possibly had an encounter with the Cryptic Killer and lived to tell her tale, both men were pleasantly surprised and somewhat taken aback when Emma opened the door.

Although dressed in her unflattering, figure concealing, light-grey sweats and oversize t-shirt, she was not what they were expecting.

She in no way resembled their preconceived image of an illegal street sex worker; haggard looking crack whores with over sized wigs, make-up that looked like it was applied in the dark with a spatula and bodies that screamed neglect. But that certainly wasn't Emma.

Jack and Spence shot a brief side-ways glance of approval as she stepped back to allow them access. Even in her stressed state, even after she had to flee for and her life and cower in fear, she was still an alluring presence. Her natural beauty was not lost on the visitors.

The agreeable aroma off freshly brewed coffee was next to welcome the boys as they entered the apartment.

She gestured towards the lounge chairs. 'Please... have a seat. I've just made a pot of coffee.' She indicated her freshly poured mug on the coffee table in front of the Detectives, who were lowering themselves onto the lounge sofa. 'Can I get you gentlemen one?' she asked.

Both men accepted the offer and a few short minutes later all three were seated in her lounge room sipping hot coffees while she opened her soul to these two complete strangers staring back at her.

Jack edged himself forward in his chair. He held Emma's gaze. 'I want you to understand...we are not interested in your nocturnal activities on the street. We are Homicide, not Vice...' Jack said.

Emma nodded her understanding as she took a sip from her coffee.

'What I want you to do, in your own time, is explain in detail
what occurred during last night.'

Emma started by telling the boys she was a law student at
NYU and her justifications for working the streets on
weekends. She told them her street pseudonym. She
mentioned where she worked, her little piece of Hudson
Street and the time she started her shift. She discussed how
the man who chased her initially tried to pick up Lulu, but
Lulu was taken by a walk-up trick. She told how her pimp
told her to pick him up on the rebound.

She told them he was a handsome man, a big man and very
charming. He was well spoken, quite eloquent actually. She
told them how he chose the location he wanted to drive to
for the service. She walked the men over to her window
overlooking the East River, peeled open her blinds and
pointed to the area where they were parked.

She told them how he sat in the passenger seat while she
knelt on the ground in front of him to perform her service on
him. She told of the sudden sharp pain in her neck and how
her wig rotated around over her face when he forcefully
twisted her head.

She lifted her lip and showed them her larger than usual eye
teeth and mentioned how one of them must have cut his
penis.

Jack and Spence just let her talk to allow her recall of every
detail to flow without interruption. Spence jotted down
notes.

Emma started to tense up when describing how she ran for her life and hid in the grounds of her apartment's estate. She told how she strategically placed clothing items on the path to lead him away from her and he eventually drove off.

'That was very clever...' Jack said when she had finished. 'Especially under extreme duress. Are you OK now...? Would you like to take a break?' He noticed she nervously rubbed and twisted her hands together.

'No, no I'm good.' She took a large hit of coffee.

'There was no intercourse, is that right?' Jack asked.

'No. He specifically asked for head... Ah, sorry. Oral,' she clarified.

Jack lifted his hand in a gesture of THAT'S OK. 'Did he ejaculate?'

'I don't think so...No, my tooth cut him before he was finished. But he was wearing a condom anyway.'

'You would have sliced open the condom...Did you happen to notice if you got any of his blood on you?' Jack asked.

'I don't think so...it was all contained in the condom...he bled into the condom.'

'Ah...right.' Jack nodded. He scratched the stubble on his chin. 'Did you see what he did with the condom when he removed it to examine his injury?' Jack asked.

Emma stared blankly. Her face remained expressionless, probably while her mind rewound back to that moment she first saw the cut on his penis.

'Um...' She lifted her closed fist. 'He held it in his hand. He rolled it up into itself, into a small roll, if you like and held in his hand.'

'What about the payment...the notes he gave you... where are they?' Jack asked.

'He gave ME his wallet and asked ME to take out my fee...said he injured his fingers and couldn't bend them or something.'

Jack's eyes flicked to Spence. 'The perp thought of every last detail. Having her remove the notes so as to mitigate any risk of leaving prints,' he said.

'Where are the clothes you wore when he attacked you?' Spence asked. 'I assume you have showered since then.' He lifted his chin her current attire.

Emma quickly jumped up and moved to her bedroom, returning a short time later with her black wig, Bolero Jacket, denim shorts and the bikini top she wore last night. She reminded the Detectives how the offender took her black thigh-high boots and cap after she planted them for him.

Emma showed the Detectives her red pair of thigh-high boots so they could get a visual image of what the black pair looked like.

Spence removed a neatly folded plastic bag, shook it open and held it out for her to place her clothing in the bag. He then sealed it shut. 'We'll get these analyzed for DNA and trace evidence and get them back to you,' he said. 'With a bit of luck there might be some blood or other evidence from him on them,' he explained.

'That's OK…I won't be needing them… I've decided to take a break for a while.'

After Emma finished updating her guests on the events from earlier in the night, she escorted the boys down to the exact location by the river where the car was earlier parked.

The brightness of a fresh new morning dominated the skyline but long dark gray shadows still stretched under the FDR, in the area of the vacant parking lot.

The Detectives conducted a detailed search of the area under probing torch lights. A check of nearby garbage bins for the discarded condom, or a blood soaked handkerchief failed to locate any evidence. Their perp was too clever to be careless, but these were stones that could not be left un-turned.

Emma then walked the boys through the grounds re-enacting both his and her movements. This time though, the horror-movie like scene of tedious black and grays in the gardens had transformed into vibrant greens and browns.

Once back in the apartment it would be another 2½ hours before they would finish compiling her statement. They required it to be completed while everything was still vivid in her mind.

Emma agreed to attend at the police station later in the day to compile a photo-fit image of her attacker. She said she would never forget his face.

By the time Jack and Spence returned to the station, Wylie had completed his photo-fit of "Bear". All they had on Wylie at this stage was four counts of aiding and abetting motor vehicle theft. There was nothing to suggest his complicity in the murders; not at this stage anyway.

The usually arrogant and opinionated Wylie was dumbstruck. He stood motionless. His face was drained of color as he stared blankly at Spence while he was informed of the consequences of his actions.

He would lose his job at the Waldorf Astoria and faced the very real possibility of jail time over the car theft charges.

Jack flicked his hand towards the door. 'Get him out of here,' Jack barked. 'I'm sick of looking at him.'

A uniform officer removed Wylie from the charge counter and escorted him to a predetermined meeting with a bail justice.

Back in the homicide Bull Pen the OPERATION CODE-BREAKER debrief was intentionally kept short. Unit Fourteen was late having been reassigned to obtain a statement from the owner of the Black Audi A6.

Jack summarized the evening and pointed out that it was through good fortune rather than good planning that the perp failed to claim his 4th victim tonight.

The crews were thanked for their cooperation and patience and were promptly dismissed so they could grab some sleep and enjoy what was left of their Sunday.

Chapter 11

Both men were pictures of concentration as they perched their butts on the side of Jack's desk. Both had their arms folded tightly across their chests and both stared intently but silently at the white board in Jack's office.

It had been four days since Emma Fisher channeled her jungle survival skills and eluded the Cryptic Killer and still they hadn't heard anything from him. No follow up letter. No further abduction attempts of street hookers. Nothing.

Jack considered the injury must have been severe enough to put him out of action for a considerable period. CK had gone off the grid.

Jack and Spence discussed how the failed murder attempt would have affected the perp. The profile THEYhad for him was that of a narcissist who didn't like to lose. With Emma eluding him, she beat him. They were uncertain how he would react. And with the humiliation of the injury she inflicted on him, it would be difficult for his personality type to accept.

Consistent with the first three murders, the perp failed to leave anything that would incriminate himself. 'The reason the perp took the clothing items left in the park by Emma was to ensure they didn't contain his DNA,' Jack explained.

Forensic examinations from the Audi A6, Emma's clothing, the surrounds of the parking lot and the vehicle recovery site all failed to locate any usable evidence. The phone the perp used to contact Wylie to arrange the vehicles was a disposable burn phone. All leads had once again hit a dead end.

All the planning, all the effort, all those man hours around the Operation and Jack still failed to expose the perp, or worse, prevent him picking up a hooker – Emma.

The photo-fit IDs from Emma and Wylie were similar in many ways. Copies had been released to the media and were being run in newspapers and TV news bulletins.

Jack also released the fact the suspect could have an injury to his groin. Anyone aware of someone with such an injury was requested to contact the police. The net was being cast wide but this guy was very, very good.

'Thank god we don't have to put Emma's picture up there,' Jack said to Spence as they continued to deliberate over the white board.

'Anyone's picture...' Spence corrected. 'Thank god we don't have to put ANYONE'Spicture up there Jobs,' Spence said. 'About time we got a break...We were well overdue,' he added.

'Yeah true...but I think it was Emma who got the break - not us...We are no closer to catching this guy,' Jack said. He lifted his chin to the whiteboard. 'I look at this board every day,' he said. 'I re-visit the evidence EVERY DAY in case there is something that I am missing and I've got nothing, Spence...absolutely nothing.'

'Don't beat yourself up Jobs... We now have a photo-fit description of what he looks like. Those distinctive sharp blue eyes. Large stature. Articulate and charismatic. Someone out there MUST know someone like that...Plus...we have not one...but two people who can positively ID him now. That's better than anything we have had before. The only ones that could ID the killer before this are looking at us from that whiteboard.'

'OK. Where to from here?' Jack asked himself, thinking out loud. Jack rubbed a hand over his chin. 'Will the killer accept a failed murder attempt...? Will he move on to a 5th letter while the 4th remains unfinished? Or will he attend to loose ends. Will he try and finish off what he started and hunt down Emma?' Jack said to himself out loud. 'You're right though Spence - She knows what he looks like. That makes her a real threat to him.'

'I can't see him sending a letter, boasting in code that he was going to kill a hooker – "CATCH ME IF YOU CAN," then try and fail. He won't be content to just walk away and leave it at that with an "OH WELL" blasé attitude... I can't see him doing that Jobs.'

'Agree...' Jack said. 'He won't just move on to letter number five like nothing happened. His credibility, his reputation, his ego have all been questioned. Imagine the embarrassment someone like him would feel. He can't send a new letter until this 4th one – Emma, is taken care of.'

'Should we put an AROUND THE CLOCK on her?' Spence asked.

'The Gnome would never approve it. We just have to make her aware that she needs to be extra careful…. She's switched on…she'll be OK.'

Jack was on a call when Spence burst into his office. He held up a finger to his visitor while he finished his call. 'Sorry 'bout that. That was the Gnome,' he said cradling the handset. 'What's up?'

'We got a hit from the photo fits we published in the media…' Spence's tone was upbeat. Jack adjusted himself in his chair in anticipation. 'A female caller claims she knows who "Bear" is…'

'Did we got a name…?'

'We did.' Spence checked his note pad. 'The caller thinks the "Bear" in the photo fit we published is a person she knows as Andre Van den Berg… 29… Lives on his own in an apartment on 19th Street, in Chelsea…'

'Any form…?'

'Nothing…clean skin. Not even a traffic infringement.'

'How can the caller be sure it's him…?'

'She dated him for a while apparently…She says she remembers his nickname was "Bear" because of his stature; she says he is about 6 feet 10 inches… as big as a grizzly bear and can be just as angry.'

'Do we know anything about him at all…?'

Spence checked his notes. 'Ah, he attended Duke on a football scholarship.' Spence 's eyes lifted from his notes. 'Not surprising I guess when you're built like that.' Spence returned to his notes. 'Let's see...she says he moved here from North Carolina for work about 3 years ago...The caller says he is very intelligent, charismatic and drop-dead gorgeous...' Spence lifted his eyes... 'I assume that means he's handsome...'

'Tick. tick. tick.' Jack said. 'What does he do...?'

'Um...' Spence flipped over a page. 'She says he's a Research Analyst on Wall Street.' Spence lifted his eyes and shrugged. 'Whatever that is...'

'Get a copy of his photo from the DMV records,' Jack said. 'Then arrange for Emma and Wylie to come in and view it...'

'On to it,' Spence said as he exited the office.

Easter was a busy time with hundreds of thousands of people migrating across the country to spend time with their families, that is, those who have someone to spend the period with.

For Jack it was just another Saturday. His de-facto family are his work colleagues but on the weekend, this Easter weekend in particular, they would all be spending time enjoying the company of their own families.

The morning was clear and fresh, with a gentle breeze blowing, swirling at times among the inner city buildings. As Jack exited his apartment building he made his obligatory assessment of the street for any perceived risks; anything out of place that could suggest an ambush.

Satisfied all was clear he glanced up at the sparse scattering of clouds and inhaled a lung full of New York air as he headed off on his morning run.

Working as a Homicide cop exposed him to some of the most dangerous and vindictive criminals in the country. Vicious street gangs the likes of MS-13, 18TH STREET GANG, BLOODS, CRIPS, and LATIN KINGS, as well as prison gangs the likes of TRINITARIOS and the ARYAN BROTHERHOOD. All were merciless people who placed no value on human life. They would not think twice at the revenge killing of the cop who incarcerated their brother, father, friend or colleague.

Jack accepted nothing in his life could be routine. Everything had to change around so his routine couldn't be established in case of contract hits. Things such as his daily run paths, when he did his shopping, the time he left for work, the time he walked home, the way he walked home, everything had to differ from the day before. His spatial awareness was sharper than most, but routine was what would get you killed in his line of work.

Today Jack opted to run down to the East River, along the bike tracks, down around Battery Point, up the Hudson bike tracks and back home. He checked at his watch. It was 9.30am. He pressed his stopwatch and sent the timer racing as he plodded off.

For Jack these runs were therapeutic. They cleared his head and oxygenated his brain. The scenery was pleasant and the endorphin release helped relieve his stress levels.

For the duration of the run at least, he forgot about the things that weighed him down. He forgot about the things that ate away at his health; things like the elusive Cryptic Killer.

For the next hour or so the only thing on his mind, apart from the music feeding through his earphones, was the rhythm of his breathing in harmony with his pacing.

Twenty minutes in and Jack had hit his rhythm. His stride was long and strong. A Velcro strap securely tethered his mobile phone to his bicep. Its music player fed his headphones with his selection of tunes to run by.

Without warning the song he sang along to was interrupted by his mobile phone cutting in and chirping in his ears.

He briefly considered answering it but decided whoever it was could wait. He wasn't on call this weekend, so they could leave a message until his run was over; this was HIStime.

Less than twenty seconds later his music was once again interrupted by the chirping of his mobile in his ears. He again ignored the call.

'Fuck me,' he said to himself, as the unforgiving tone of his phone chirped in his ear for a third time. IT MUST BE IMPORTANT FOR SOMEONE TO RING THREE TIMES AND NOT LEAVE A MESSAGE.Jack took the call, while he continued to jog. 'Jack Head,' he puffed.

'Thank God Jack I've been trying to get you all morning...'
The clearly distressed voice on the other end exclaimed.

Jack frowned. 'Lynnie...?' Jack asked. Although now
divorced, he knew every one of her emotions learned from
over twenty-eight years of marriage. This one worried him.
The obvious distress in her voice was serious. He stopped
running. 'Everything OK?' His eyes darted. He could hear
crying on the other end of his phone. 'Lynnie, for God's sake
what's wrong...? Are you alright?' he asked.

'It's Maxie, Jack...he's...he's...' Her voice broke down as she
became overcome by emotion. Her body shuddered and
prevented her from articulating any discernible words.

The two uniformed officers who came knocking at her door
had just delivered the most devastating news; news that
every parent dreaded. Their somber faces expressed more
than any spoken words to her could; the only question
was WHO...?

'What about him...Lynnie...What about Max?' Jack asked.
The pit of his stomach grew heavy.

'He's dead Jack...He's dead,' she blurted.

Jack's mouth fell open. His shoulders slumped. The color
instantly drained from his face. He stared blankly ahead.
'What are you talking about? How?' Was all he could muster
as his words jammed around the lump forming in his throat.

'Car accident... They said he was passenger in a car that
collided with a truck. He's gone Jack...He's gone and he's

never coming back... Oh my God... Oh God,' her voice faded off.

Jack stumbled to the side of the track. His legs struggled to hold his weight. He unknowingly crossed in front of other track users, unaware of the evil glares he received as they were forced to take evasive action to avoid colliding with him.

His eyes were fixed into a blank stare. His face was devoid of any discernible emotion while the sounds of Lynne's heart wrenching cries resonated through his earphones.

Although estranged from his family for many years, Max was still his son, his oldest boy. He was still the same son that tiny bundle of joy he so proudly cradled in arms, wrapped tightly in the securing comfort of a blanket only minutes after he entered the world. The son who was an adult version of the little boy smiling so happily in the picture he so proudly carried in his wallet.

Jack swallowed hard. He took a breath. 'Where was the accident Lynne...? Are you there?'

'California...' Caitlyn said. 'He was only over there for work Jack,' she said. 'He was only over there for work...'

This was too much for him to process; a death message over the telephone. It didn't seem real. It didn't seem true. Jack rubbed a hand across his mouth. His face filled with lines of concern. 'I'm coming over...I'll be there as soon as I can,' Jack said.

Years of investigating murders, some bodies too gruesome to recall, never worried Jack, it was all part of the job. It was always someone else's family. But the thought of one of his own family – his son, tore at him.

The thought of him lying there with a "Y" shaped incision on the chest of his pale and lifeless body broke Jack. The impenetrable facade Jack had erected over all these years now started to show signs of cracks.

His eyes started to well up. It was a feeling he had not experienced since he was a small boy, so he fought to fight it off, to conceal it, in case he was noticed by anyone showing weakness.

Jack was raised by a tough disciplinarian. His father was a giant of a man, not unlike Jack's build and he was tough to Jack and his three brothers. He was a laborer, a man's-man, who believed it was a sign of weakness for a man to show emotion- ANY emotion.

"REAL MEN DON'T CRY AND THEY DON'T SHOW FEAR, BOY". His Father's words still resonated after all these years.

When disciplined, if Jack or his brothers cried as young boys, his father would always say, "YOU GUNNA CRY ARE YA...? THEN I'LL GIVE YOU SOMETHING TO CRY ABOUT" and he would hit them again - only harder. They learned very quickly to suppress their emotions.

His Dad always said "FATHER'S DON'T HUG THEIR SONS COZ MEN DON'T EMBRACE OTHER MEN, UNLESS THEY'RE HOMOSEXUAL. THEY SHAKE HANDS AND THEY SHAKE HANDS FIRMLY – LIKE A MAN".

Years of this narrow-minded way of thinking and mental abuse taught Jack to conceal his true feelings. He learned to hide ANY emotion, happy or sad, to avoid incurring the condescending wrath of his father.

Jack's father didn't see it as abuse. It was the way HISFather brought HIM up, and HE turned out alright, or
so HE thought. It was the way a Father should bring his boys up. It was the only way Jack's Father knew how to turn his boys into men – real men.

Unfortunately for Jack, all this suppression and concealment of emotion he had developed through his youthful years contributed to the failing of his marriage and the estrangement from his boys.

He loved them with every piece of his being, but his father made sure he stripped Jack of the ability to show it. He stripped Jack of the ability to let them know he loved them unconditionally. In the case of his boys, they simply had no idea because Jack didn't know how to show it.

The front door swung open and Caitlyn flung herself at Jack. She wrapped her arms around him and nestled her head into his large chest as she let it all out. She cried so hard her body bounced in his arms.

Jack fought hard to stave off his own tears. He couldn't cry in front of Lynne. He had to be strong. But his emotions gurgled inside him, like a volcano waiting to erupt.

A few shots of whiskey each and a strong coffee later and Caitlyn and Jack sat in her lounge room discussing the circumstances of the accident, as relayed to her by the police.

'How's Dan handling it?' Jack asked.

'He's devastated. He's lost his best mate. He looked up to Maxie, Jack.' Caitlyn's eyes lifted to Jack. 'Please don't take this the wrong way...but Maxie was the father figure Danny never had.' Jack's head fell forward. Her frank honesty cut close.

'Where is he now?' Jack asked.

'He's staying at his girlfriend's place.' She dabbed her eyes with the drenched tissue she had scrunched up in her hand. All Jack could do was nod his understanding.

Jack stayed with Caitlyn most of the night to keep her company. He wouldn't admit it to himself, but he also stayed so he too had company.

Caitlyn regaled Jack with anecdotal tales of the happier times with Max. Sadly, they were all new stories to Jack. It was as though he listened to stories about someone else's child.

She talked about her happy memories from before and after the marriage split.

It was all they talked about-- Max's short life. Whether they realized or not it was therapeutic for the both of them.

Chapter 12

Since Max's funeral Jack maintained regular contact with Caitlyn, visiting her when he was able. She welcomed his support and attention. She joked that she had seen more of Jack in the weeks since poor Maxie's tragic death than she did through twenty-eight years of marriage.

It was late afternoon and Jack had taken time out from his pursuit of the Cryptic Killer to take the drive out to Maplewood to see how Caitlyn was. They sat on her back porch drinking strong coffee and just being there for one another.

'I have a really big favor to ask of you Jack.' Caitlyn appeared nervous. She held her coffee mug in two hands. 'Please say no, if you don't want to do it, but it would mean a lot to me.' She sipped her coffee.

'Sure. Just name it.' He sipped his coffee.

'I told Max's landlord what had happened and he said that he would obviously void the remaining rental agreement. But he asked me if I could have all Max's possessions cleaned out before the rent expired in two weeks. Of course I agreed to do it.'

'OK,' Jack said. 'Do you want a hand?'

'No...' Caitlyn firmly shook her head. 'I was hoping that YOU could do it for me. I don't think I could go there and pack up all his property, Jack. It would just kill me. It's too final...All his possessions,' she shook her lowered head. 'I was hoping you could do it for me, if it isn't too much trouble.' Her pained eyes lifted to Jack

'No problem Lynne.' He placed a comforting hand over hers. 'I'll go there this weekend and get a start.'

'Thank you so much. You have no idea how much that means to me,' she said. Her face wore a genuine smile of relief and gratitude. 'I'll have the storage boxes delivered, they'll be there waiting for you.'

She reached into her pocket. 'This is the landlord's business card with his number and this is Max's front door key and his address in Rumson.' She paused and stared silently at the key in her hand for several seconds, then passed the key to Jack.

Spence arrived at Jack's office door and paused when he noticed Jack sitting at his desk with a blank stare. Jack didn't notice Spence in the doorway.

The Gnome told Jack to take whatever time off he needed to recover from the tragic loss of his son. But true to form, Jack waved it off and attended for work as normal. But everything was far from normal for Jack.

The events of the last few weeks had been a distraction for Jack. He had not dedicated quality time to the Cryptic Killer case since Max's passing. His mind was firmly on the memory of his son he never really knew.

He tried to recall events from Max's life, things they shared together and as a family but the cupboard was bare.

The stark realization hit home. His boy was gone and he never spent any quality time with him. He didn't really know him. He had no memories. He had nothing to keep Max's memory alive and that devastated him.

'Jobs...?' Spence said gently.

Jack eyes slowly moved towards Spence. His expression was still frozen. He held the blank stare for a few short seconds, then his eyebrows arched upwards when he noticed Spence at the door. 'Spence...didn't see you there - come in.' He motioned towards the visitor's chair. 'What's happening?' Jack said.

Spence moved to sit in the chair opposite Jack. 'Are you going down to Rumson this weekend?' Spence said.

'Yeah,' Jack said. His nodding head lowered. He straightened some pens on his desk. 'I'm planning to go down there this weekend to get a start on packing up Max's stuff for Lynnie.'

Spence clapped his hands together and rubbed them eagerly. 'Do you want a hand big fellow,' Spence said. 'I have nothing planned. We could knock it over together.'

'Thanks Spence...But you know what...?' Jack began. 'I really think I need to do this on my own. It's just something I have to do. You understand.'

Spence raised both hands to Jack. 'Hey, no problems Jobs. Just sing out if you need any help... I'm only a phone call away.'

'Much appreciated,' Jack said. He wasn't used to these emotional feelings churning inside of him. He fought to suppress them. These were feelings of gratitude, of being touched by the genuine caring friendship and support of his close friend. A lifetime of burying these feelings deep inside was now being eroded by the tragic passing of Max.

'Hey...' Spence began in an upbeat tone... 'You up for some news about our killer... Or would you rather park it for a while...?'

'No I'm good. Whatcha got?'

'Hang on...' Spence ran back to his desk, returning a few seconds later. He handed Jack a 10 by 8 inch color photograph. 'This just came in...That there is our man...that is "Bear".'

Jack accepted the photo and examined it. The head and shoulders shot of Andre Van den Berg stared back at him through piercing blue eyes. His hair was shaved short. His chiseled jaw was supported by a thick, strong neck.

Finally... a breakthrough. Could this really be a photo of his elusive Cryptic Killer? 'How did we go with getting in touch with the witnesses...Emma and Wylie. We need to show this to them ASAP, to confirm he's our guy.' Jack said.

'All done. I called them up and they are both coming in on Saturday to look at the photo. I'll leave a copy down at the front counter with uniform to show them when they attend.'

'Good. We also need to find out if this guy has an injury to his pecker...' Jack said.

'We have already checked with the hospitals and medical centers...and nobody has presented with such an injury...' Spence said.

Jack rubbed a contemplative hand across his chin. 'We've gotta bring him in, Spence.' Jack checked his notes. 'Do we know what firm he works for?'

Spence shook his head. 'No, the caller didn't know.'

'Looks like we're heading down to Chelsea to see what we can find out about this guy...' Jack said lifting the photo up to Spence.

Jack pushed himself from his chair and moved to his whiteboard where he positioned the photo of "Bear" at the top of the whiteboard, above the photo of the victims. He stepped back and viewed his work in silence.

When he was done he wrenched open his desk top drawer and removed his car keys. 'Let's go,' he said.

During the 20 minute drive to Chelsea both men discussed the prospects about how they could be on the verge to finally capturing their elusive killer. Their leads were hot and the information they received appeared credible.

Van den Berg's description matched Emma's description of her attacker. His physical size and the "Bear" nickname matched the information provided by Wylie. It was slowly coming together.

Jack parked in an available space about 5 doors down from Van den Berg's apartment building and they made their way back. The street-level entry to the renovated warehouse building was locked.

Jack examined the wall-mounted intercom. Some buttons provided an occupant's name while others only provided an apartment number. He pressed the button marked 12-- the apartment number provided for Van den Berg by their female caller.

His curious eyes met Spence when there was no response. He pressed the button a 2nd time with the same result. Jack stepped back and ran his eyes up the face of the building, trying to estimate the apartment numbers.

'There's a button here for the building Super, Jack...' Spence said. He pressed the button.

'Can I help you...' a curt voice replied.

Spence moved closer to the intercom. 'Yes, I was hoping you can. My name is Detective Sergeant Spencer...I am from New York Homicide. I was hoping to talk to you about one of your residents in the apartment building.' Spence's gaze shifted to Jack when there was no immediate response. He frowned. 'Are you there?'

After a few seconds beat by the voice replied, 'I'm here...I'm just not sure how I can help you though...I don't know anything about any homicide...'

'Are you the building super...?' Spence asked.

'I am.'

'We were hoping to discuss one of your residents...Could you buzz us in please, so we can talk to you.'

'Wait there. I'll come up.'

Following a wait of about 3 minutes an electronic buzz emanated before the solid timber door opened. A short male in his early sixties peeped around the partially open door, with the door resting his shoulder. His thinning gray hair and ruddy complexion stared back at Jack and Spence.

'How can I help?'

Jack slipped the photo of Van den Berg from his folder and held it up. 'Have you seen this man before?' Jack asked.

The man examined the photograph. 'I have...'

'Do you know who he is?'

'What's he supposed to have done...?' The man asked as his inquiring eyes flicked between Jack and Spence.

'We are not saying he's done anything... We are just making routine inquiries at this time,' Jack said. He pushed the photo forward. 'Do you know his name?'

The man's questioning eyes flicked between each man as he regarded Jack and Spence. 'How do I know you guys are cops?'

Both men slipped out their badges and presented them to the super. He individually examined each badge. 'OK...you just never know these days...' he said.

'How do you know this guy in the photo?' Jack asked.

'That's Andre... He used to live in apartment 12. Really nice guy. I think they call him bear coz he's a big mother fucker... Is he in some kind of trouble...?'

'Used to live in apartment 12...' Jack repeated, ignoring the question.

'Yeah... he moved out a while back.'

'How long ago did he move...?'

'Coupla months, I s'pose.'

'Do you have a forwarding address?'

He shook his head. 'Sorry. I don't. He comes by every now and then to collect any mail sent here to his old address, though.'

'When did you last see him?'

'Gee...' The man lifted his eyes skyward. 'It'd have to be a coupla weeks now...' he said.

'Do you know where he works...?'

'No...I don't, sorry.'

'What about a contact number for him..?'

He shook his head. 'Sorry.'

Jack had heard enough. The super was little help so he thanked him for his time and they returned to their vehicle. All Jack could focus on was how his person of interest continues to elude them.

'Do you believe him Spence...?'

'Believe he doesn't know anything...?' Spence clarified. He didn't wait for a response. 'Hard to say Jobs... I think so...But having said that I wouldn't be surprised if he is protecting Van den Berg though...'

'I think he knows more than he's letting on...'

'We'll get him, Jack,' Spence reassured as they strolled. 'Once we find out where Van den Berg works...we'll get him. Why don't we get the media's help on this one... you know, have them ask if anyone knows him, or ask for him to come forward...'

Jack nodded. 'Good idea...Can you arrange that, Spence...I've got a few things on my mind at the moment?'

'Got it, Jobs. Leave it to me. Have you thought anymore about whether you need any help this weekend?'

'Thanks Spence...but I think I need to do it on my own,' Jack said. Deep down he didn't want Spence around in case he couldn't control his emotions while he cleaned out Max's things.

Chapter 13

Max's house overlooked the beach in the picturesque coastal area of Rumson, New Jersey. The narrow single fronted, two-story weatherboard house was tastefully presented.

The chocolate milk tones of the weatherboards were complimented by fresh contrasting white eaves and trims around the windows and doors, while white balustrades stretched across the width of the house on the upstairs balcony. Small white pebbles replaced lawn in the low maintenance front yard.

Jack unlocked the front door and slowly stepped inside. The uninhabited house that was once his son's private retreat had an eerie solitude to it.

He moved to his left and entered Max's lounge room where he stood for a moment taking in a typical first-time look around the room.

Luckily Max's lease was for a fully furnished house, so most of the furniture in here belonged to the landlord; no heavy lifting and no moving vans.

As he surveyed the small lounge room a wave of sadness engulfed him. It dawned on him that he stood in his son's home, his sanctuary and it's a place to which he had never been invited. He never knew anything about his oldest boy's life.

Jack noticed the extensive collection of framed photos proudly displayed in various vantage points around the room. Jack moved from photograph to photograph. He took the time to examine the captured moments depicting happier times in Max's life.

Some photos pictured a happy Max on his own smiling down the camera lens, while others were of Max and his friends that Jack never knew.

He smiled proudly when he noticed a recent framed photograph of his two boys, Max and Dan standing with their arms around each other, both holding a thumb up to the camera.

He paused when he noticed a number of photographs in close proximity. Each one depicted Max, Dan and Caitlyn, all smiling, all happy.

It wasn't until Jack noticed the photographs of Max with his elderly grandparents – Caitlyn's mom and dad – and how these photos took pride of place on his lounge room mantle that the harsh reality hit home.

These were Max's treasured pictorial memories on display. All the photographs adorning the walls, mantelpiece, coffee table and side tables were Max's special memories depicting important people in his life that HE chose to frame and proudly display.

Yet Jack wasn't depicted in any of them. He was the glaring absentee from every one of the photos. He had been estranged for so long he wasn't even a faint memory to Max. Clearly to Max, Jack was never a part of his life. Not even one small photo in his extensive lounge room collection. That was a tough reality for any father to rationalize.

Jack paused to examine the two framed degrees hanging side-by-side on the lounge room wall, each one bearing Max's name. All this time he never knew Max had achieved a double degree in Law and Criminology.

The pain he felt in not being able to share in Max's achievements hit hard and now it's too late.

The flat-packs that had to be opened out and assembled into boxes to pack Max's property into lay in bundles in the hall beside the stairs, waiting for Jack's arrival.

Jack started with the ground floor and moved room-by-room placing everything that was once Max's possessions into a box and tightly sealed it with duct tape.

Once he completed the downstairs he moved to the upstairs bedrooms where he followed the same ritual. Everything that once showed Max's tastes, preferences, personality and his presence in the house was all carefully packed away and sealed in a cardboard box.

After the last box from upstairs had been brought down and placed with the others at the front door, Jack did a sweep of the house to check he hadn't missed anything.

Although fully furnished, the house was now devoid of all the personality it had previously boasted. The photos, the nick-knacks, all the little possessions that made it Max's home were now gone. Only a blank canvass remained, waiting in readiness for the next tenant to decorate and characterize to suit their individual tastes.

After checking he had everything, Jack returned to the front entry foyer. He was satisfied he had gathered everything. All that was once reflective of his son's life was now neatly sealed in the boxes piling up at his feet at the front door.

As Jack stood in the entry foyer running through a mental check list, he noticed a door under the staircase. He rolled his eyes. THE BASEMENT.

Jack opened the basement door. The natural light from the hall bled down the stairs and blended into the darkness below.

He flicked on the light. A single globe dangled from a cord above the stairs. The light was dull, but enough to show the way. He commenced to make his way down the stairs into the basement. The timber treads creaked as his towering frame shifted over them.

The air was dense and much cooler in the basement and there was a musty odor. The basement stored minimal property, all of which fitted neatly into one single box.

Jack dragged the last of the duct tape over the top of the box and sealed it. As he lifted his eyes from the last box he noticed the small room tucked away in the corner of the basement. The door was locked with a large pad lock. WAS THAT A ROOM WHERE THE LANDLORD STORED HIS OWN POSSESSIONS UNDER LOCK AND KEY, OR WAS IT MAX'S ROOM?

He slipped the landlord's business card from his pocket and called the landlord, just to be sure he wasn't leaving anything behind. The landlord confirmed the room and its contents belonged to the tenant.

Jack held the large padlock in his hand. He glanced around the basement wondering where Max would keep a spare key. His searching eyes scanned around the many nooks and likely hiding places in the basement. WHERE WOULD I HIDE A KEY DOWN HERE IF IT WERE ME?

Jack's eyes locked onto the timber stairs. The light from the open doorway above still bled down the stairs into the basement. It was a brighter source of light than the dull globe hanging above the stairs.

Jack made his way to the darkened underside of the timber stairs and commenced to search for a key. But there was nothing.

Jack rubbed a hand across his mouth. He was about to concede when his focus locked onto on the bottom tread, which was about six inches off the ground. THAT'S WHERE I'D PUT IT.

With nothing to lose, Jack knelt down and swept his hand back-and-forth under the tread. His hand hit something. It was a key taped to the underneath of the last step. Jack peeled off the key and examined it.

The padlock offered no resistance to Jack when he slid in the key and turned it. The lock sprung open. The outwards opening door creaked as Jack peeled it open to reveal a small room in total darkness.

Jack ducked his head under the low door way and moved into the darkness of the unknown room. He looked around for a light switch, while his eyes adjusted to the darkness.

Jack squinted when he flicked on the light. His eyes took a moment to adjust to the dull light. He scanned the small room for any personal possessions. A laptop, a desk lamp and printer were the first items he noticed. Jack's wandering gaze shifted to his left. His eyebrows dipped. He leaned his hands on the small desk while he examined the wall above the desk.

The entire wall was plastered with newspaper articles — each one about him. Some dated as far back as ten years. WHY DID MAX HAVE ALL THESE ARTICLES ABOUT ME, YET HE COULDN'T PUT ONE PICTURE OF ME IN HIS LOUNGE?MAYBE HE WAS SECRETLY PROUD OF MY ACHIEVEMENTS BUT DIDN'T WANT TO SHOW IT TO THE REST OF HIS FAMILY. Jack slowly shook his head as his eyes moved from article to article.

He searched the room for any of Max's property. He started with the desk drawers. The first drawer contained a box of latex gloves. Jack raised a curious eyebrow.

As he slid the next drawer open his heart skipped a beat. Tucked away in this drawer was a ream of lemon yellow paper . Beside it was a packet of lemon yellow envelopes. Jack pulled his hand back from the drawer, as if it burned his hand.

He stared in disbelief at the open drawer. He rubbed a heavily perspiring hand across his mouth and chin as he scanned the room. His eyes locked onto the newspaper wall. 'What the fuck's going on here?'

Jack lifted the screen of the laptop computer and started it up. The boot up process stalled at the password login screen. 'Shit,' he said, then slammed the screen shut.

Jack continued to search the desk. In a desk caddy cluttered with pens and other stationery items he noticed a mobile phone SIM card stored in a small transparent plastic holder. After briefly studying the SIM he slid it into his pocket.

Jack fell back into the chair with his hands clasped behind his head and stared at the wall. Max wasn't secretly proud of him at all. Jack's eyes flared with realization. 'Fuck,' Jack said. His eyes dropped to the laptop in front of him. He had to check the contents of that laptop.

Jack reached down and one-by-one opened the remaining drawers and checked their contents. He no longer searched for Max's property to box up, he now looked for answers.

Jack stood from his chair and started ripping at the newspaper articles on the wall. They had to go. One-by-one he ripped them down and dropped them onto the desk. He paused when the removal of one news article exposed a white envelope pinned to the wall. The word "Mom" was hand written on the front.

Jack unpinned the sealed envelope from the wall and sat back in the chair. His eyes never left the envelope in his hand. He held it up to the light. It appeared to contain a folded up piece of paper. He could make out typed writing on the paper inside. He placed it on the desk and stared at the envelope, almost too frightened to open it; too frightened for what it might contain.

Jack scanned the room again. He scanned the remaining newspaper articles on the wall in front of him, then back at the envelope. He stood and peeled off every other newspaper article, in case there were any other hidden messages. But the wall was bare.

Jack dropped back to his seat. He rubbed his brow as he stared at the envelope on the desk. It was addressed to Caitlyn but he had to open it. He had no choice. He lifted up the envelope and flipped it over to examine the back. He exhaled heavily, paused and then ripped it open. He glanced inside before sliding out the single piece of white paper.

His mouth was dry. His temple throbbed. He slowly unfolded the letter and started to read. His worst nightmares had just become his reality.

DEAR MOM

IF YOU ARE READING THIS LETTER IT MEANS THAT I AM PROBABLY DEAD, MORE THAN LIKELY SHOT BY THE POLICE.

I HAVE WRITTEN THIS LETTER TO YOU SO YOU CAN UNDERSTAND WHY I DID WHAT I DID.

I COULD NO LONGER SIT BY IDLY AND WATCH HOW THAT MAN YOU CALLED YOUR HUSBAND IGNORED YOU - IGNORED US. HOW HE PUT HIS WORK BEFORE HIS FAMILY. IT WAS A DISGRACE. I SAW HOW UPSET YOU WERE WHEN HE DIDN'T COME HOME AT NIGHTS. YOU THOUGHT YOU WERE BEING DISCREET, BUT I SAW YOU CRYING WHEN HE MISSED YOUR ANNIVERSARIES, OR FAMILY EVENTS. I SAW YOUR DISAPPOINTMENT AND WHAT THE PSYCHOLOGICAL ABUSE AND TORMENT WAS DOING TO YOUR HEALTH AND YOUR SANITY, AND IT WAS KILLING ME. IT WAS EATING AWAY AT ME FROM THE INSIDE. I FELT SO HELPLESS. I HATED HIM WITH ALL MY BEING. I DESPISED HIM FOR WHAT HE WAS DOING TO YOU.

WHO DID HE THINK HE WAS? HE WAS AN ARROGANT MAN WHO PLACED MORE INTEREST IN SOLVING A CRIME THAN SPENDING PRECIOUS TIME WITH HIS FAMILY. HE NEVER GAVE DAN OR ME ANY TIME. HE DIDN'T CARE ABOUT US, ABOUT ANY OF US. HIS WORK ALWAYS CAME FIRST. CATCHING CRIMINALS CAME FIRST. HIS REPUTATION CAME FIRST. HE WAS ONLY HAPPY IF HE SOLVED A CASE AND IF HE DIDN'T, IF HE COULDN'T, HE WAS HELL TO BE AROUND.

WELL MOM, I COULDN'T TAKE IT ANYMORE, SITTING BY AND WATCHING WHAT HE DID TO YOU; TO ALL OF US. I SIMPLY WON'T TAKE IT ANYMORE. I KNEW THAT IF HE HAD A MURDER CASE THAT HE COULDN'T SOLVE, IT WOULD EAT AWAY AT HIM AND EAT AWAY AT HIM IN SUCH A WAY THAT IT WOULD BREAK HIM MENTALLY. I WOULD LOVE TO BREAK HIM PHYSICALLY, LORD KNOWS I'M MORE THAN CAPABLE,

BUT THAT WOULDN'T DO. BUT THIS WAY, HE IS SO FOCUSED ON HIS JOB HE COULD NOT ACCEPT LOSING, HE COULD NOT ACCEPT THAT THE GREAT JACK HEAD FAILED TO SOLVE A CASE, OR FAILED TO SAVE HIS VICTIM. I KNOW HE COULD NOT LIVE WITH HIMSELF. I HAD TO PSYCHOLOGICALLY BEAT HIM INTO A BLITHERING MESS, WHERE HE WAS UNFIT TO HOLD A BADGE.

I DON'T EXPECT YOU TO UNDERSTAND THE EXTENTS THAT I HAVE GONE TO BUT YOU HAVE TO KNOW AND UNDERSTAND THAT I DID IT FOR YOU; FOR US. HE COULDN'T PUT HIS FAMILY AHEAD OF HIS WORK, SO IF I DO THIS RIGHT, IT WILL BE THE VERY THING HE CHERISHED MORE THAN HIS FAMILY THAT WILL BE HIS UNDOING. IT WILL BE HIS WORK THAT WILL BE HIS DEMISE. IF I DO THIS RIGHT JACK HEAD WILL IMPLODE.

I HOPE YOU CAN FORGIVE ME BUT I COULDN'T SEE ANY OTHER WAY TO MAKE HIM ACCOUNTABLE FOR THE ABUSE AND HELL HE HAS PUT US ALL THROUGH.

I LOVE YOU MOM

MAX.

Jack's mouth fell open. He dropped the letter onto the desk and buried his head into his hands. He could not believe what he read. The person he had grown to despise, the vermin who brazenly killed young hookers, the person he longed for the day he could look him in the eyes as he was being led away...The CRYPTIC KILLER...was his son.

The killer was the son he had grieved for over for the last two-weeks. The son he wished he had taken the time to get to know better.

The irony was not lost on Jack. Max resented Jack for investigating violent killers, instead of spending time with his family. Yet Max had become one of those very same people who kept Jack from his family all those years ago. He could not believe it had come to this.

Jack sat for several minutes while he composed himself. The melting pot of emotions he experienced was consuming: Anger; disappointment, shock, embarrassment, regret, denial and disbelief. But despite the feelings churning inside of him, he couldn't bring himself to hate his boy for what he did. He was his boy and now he felt responsible.

With the exception of the laptop and the letter, Jack placed everything else from the small room into a box and sealed it. On the outside of the box, in thick black permanent marker he wrote "PROPERTY OF JACK HEAD" so it wouldn't be confused with Max's boxes.

Jack took the laptop with him, but secured the box in the store room for safe keeping.

For Jack, the Cryptic Killer investigation had taken a devastating twist. What was intended as an act of goodwill to box up Max's possessions for Caitlyn, turned into the worse discovery of evidence for Jack.

But like a true investigator, he refused to accept anything on face value. He refused to leave any stone un-turned. He needed irrefutable, conclusive evidence before he accepted his own son was capable of such atrocities, as desperate as that seemed.

Monday morning was like any other morning in the Homicide bull pen. Detectives with vague expressions staring through weary eyes, sipped on fresh hot coffees. But for Jack, his focus was the case and his recent findings.

To Jack, being able to access Max's laptop computer was crucial. He was certain there would be something of value on it that would assist with his investigation, but he didn't have the skills necessary to by-pass the boot-up password.

He decided to visit the Computer Forensics Team to seek their assistance. In the hope he would receive some sympathy, Jack told his colleagues the laptop was his late son's and he was in the process of finalizing his son's financial affairs and needed access to his password protected laptop.

The Forensic analyst, Roger was indeed sympathetic to Jack. He was more than happy to offer advice.

'There are a couple of methods you could use...' Roger said. 'The first involves using the Universal BIOS password, or alternatively, you could clear the CMOS and return all setups to default. Both methods will usually work.'

Jack stared blankly at the analyst. His mouth fell open as he slowly shook his head. 'I have no idea what you just said,' Jack said. 'Is there any way you could have a look at it for me?' Jack said.

'We're not supposed to do non-official work here Jobs...'
Roger said. He briefly held Jack's gaze. He shrugged. 'But
you know what... fuck it, it's for your late son. Leave it with
me.' He slipped Jack a sly wink. 'I'll see what I can do.'

Final Chapter

The SIM card Jack found in Max's basement storeroom was
next to face his scrutiny. The mobile phone TELCO he
contacted instructed him to place the unknown SIM into
another mobile phone and then send a text message from
that phone, to another phone. The receiving phone will show
the number of the sending phone.

So as to keep his inquiries private, Jack decided to borrow
Spence's mobile phone. He told Spence that he was having
trouble with the SIM card in his own phone and wanted to
test it in another phone. Spence willingly obliged without
any questions.

Jack placed Max's SIM card into Spence's phone, snapped
the back closed and sent himself a text message from
Spence's phone.

Jack stared impatiently at the phone on the desk in front of
him, waiting for the text message to come through. Within

seconds his phone started vibrating. His SMS tone alerted him that a message had been received.

'Sounds like it's working now,' Spence yelled from his desk.

'Yeah… must be my phone Spence,' Jack yelled back.

Jack slipped on his reading glasses. His heart sank when he compared it to the phone number Brenton Wylie had listed in his phone under the contact name, "BEAR". The numbers were an exact match. Max was "Bear."

Jack slumped back into his chair. The pit of his stomach was heavy. Jack slowly shook his disbelieving head.

He replaced Spence's SIM card and returned the phone to Spence. 'Thanks for that.' He placed the phone on the desk in front of Spence. 'I think I might have to get a new phone.'

Jack had one last piece of the puzzle he needed. His next inquiry was to verify which California police department attended Max's fatal car accident.

Jack's interrogation of the Police database indicated that it was the police from Long Beach California who were responsible for the accident reports.

The Long Beach Police switch was busy when Jack phoned. After patiently waiting on hold for several minutes he identified himself and was connected through to the officer responsible for reporting the accident to the coroner.

'I understand that you attended a fatal motor vehicle accident several weeks back— car versus truck — in which a male person was killed.'

'That's correct. How can I help you?'

'The young man who was killed was my son, Max.'

'I am so sorry for your loss, Detective.'

'I'm looking for a huge favor.'

'Sure.'

'I was hoping to sight a copy of the autopsy report.'

'Really? For what purpose?' the officer asked.

'Have you ever lost a child...? Jack asked.

'No. Fortunately I have not.'

'You know what us cops are like, we have to know everything,' Jack said. 'Look. It will help me personally with closure. I will know his official injuries; what he died of, etc. Can you help me out here – cop to cop,' Jack channeled his best grieving parent voice.

'Look, I'm not supposed to release official documents...' the Cop said. A long pause followed. 'You know what? Fuck it,' the cop blurted. 'If it was my kid, I'd wanna know too...and

you're a cop anyway…You got a fax number?' The officer
asked.

Five minutes later, while Jack hovered over the fax machine,
his report from Long Beach arrived.

'What ya got Jobs…? Spence asked 'You on to something…?'

'Just following a hunch Spence. Probably nothing,' Jack said.
He scooped up the report and disappeared back into his
office.

Jack slipped on his reading glasses and commenced to read
the report. He was like an over eager, but tentative student
who had just received his final exam results.

His eyes scanned over the first page. What he looked for
wasn't there. He quickly moved to page two. His eyes darted
back and forth across the page, not reading but searching.
Not there either.

He turned to the last page of the autopsy report where he
stopped scanning and started to read the information
under "SCARS, TATTOOS AND OTHER IDENTIFYING
MARKS."

"THE VICTIM HAD WHAT APPEARED TO BE A HEALED
¾ INCH LACERATION APPROXIMATELY 1½ INCHES
BELOW THE GLANS ON HIS PENIS. THE WOUND HAD
HEALED TO FORM A FRESH SCAR SUGGESTING A
RECENT INJURY."

Jack removed his reading glasses and flopped back into his chair. He glanced to the whiteboard, to the three girls staring back at him. They were there because of HIS son. He was not able to save them because HIS son had some twisted vendetta against his own father - for simply doing his job.

He rested his head in his hands. It was practically a FAIT ACCOMPLI. Jack had sufficient evidence to confirm Max WAS the CRYPTIC KILLER. There was not a jury in the country that wouldn't convict, if faced with the strength of this evidence.

He had Max's confessional letter to his mother — albeit unsigned. He had the lemon yellow paper and envelope, which he was confident when analysed, would be a match to the three previous cryptic letters. He had the printer which could be analysed to match the fonts in the letters.

He had the SIM card from the burn phone that was used to contact Wylie to arrange luxury cars, the last of which included the Audi in which Max used to pick up Emma Fisher.

He had the autopsy report recording the injury caused to his penis, which placed him in the car with Emma Fisher. He had the physical description from the two witnesses, who would both be able to identify Max from recent photos.

He now knows Max was a qualified Criminologist which explained his knowledge of crime scenes and law enforcement. The evidence was ALMOST water tight.

The passing of Max also explained why he hadn't heard from the killer since Emma Fisher's fortunate escape. Max must have gone to California for work, after the injury.

Jack's head remained in his hands. He was flattened, physically and mentally. It was all too surreal. WHAT DO I TELL MAX'S MOTHER? HOW DO I TELL HER?

'You OK jobs?' Spence asked.

Jack lifted his head to Spence standing in the doorway. Jack's expression was somber, as though another family member had passed away and he had just received the grim news. 'I'm OK Spence.' He said as he lifted the Coroner's report and folded it up.

'Well, you look like shit,' Spence said. 'I'm worried about you buddy...You should take some time off...go and spend some time with Caitlyn,' Spence suggested. 'Lean on one another for support.'

'You're right, I probably should,' Jack said. 'But we've got this prick to catch first.' He tilted his head towards the whiteboard.

Spence glanced at the whiteboard. 'He's gone to ground Jobs. Evaporated. But there's still hope... I'm waiting to catch up with Emma and Wylie to confirm the photo of Van den Berg matches our perp.'

Jack nodded. 'fingers crossed, hey...'

It had taken over two hours but Roger from Computer Forensics by-passed the boot-up log in password screen on Max's laptop. The files could now be examined.

Jack collected the laptop from Forensics and quickly returned to his office.

Back at his desk Jack searched for any files that may contain the cryptic letters he suspected Max had prepared but he couldn't locate them. Every key word he searched for came up empty. He had no choice but to visit every folder and individually examine its contents.

After about thirty minutes of fruitless searching Jack started to question that maybe Max didn't prepare the letters. He moved to an unlikely folder named "IRS RETURNS" and opened it.

There were four files inside this folder and each file had an unusual file name. He first selected the file named, "A WARNING TO PLAYERS" and opened it.

Jack donned his reading glasses and read the open document on the laptop screen. He stopped suddenly after reading the first sentence. His shoulders slumped and his head lolled forward. His aching heart prevented him from reading on.

After a few moments to compose himself, he slowly lifted his eyes back to the screen. Was the pain in his chest normal? Was it grief, or was it disappointment and disbelief? It just couldn't be – His own son.

Jack had just opened the file that contained the 4th letter he received from the Cryptic Killer. Jack checked the file properties. His blank stare locked onto the date and time stamps that verified the document was created on "WEDNESDAY 28TH MARCHby MAX HEAD."

He reluctantly opened the three remaining files in the same folder, knowing full well what he would encounter. With each file he opened, it was like another piece of his heart died. As expected, the remaining three files were Cryptic letters one to three that Jack had previously received. The document properties for each file verified they were created by Max and the chronology fitted exactly.

It was a now a water tight case against his son. Once again Jack Head had his man. Normally, after solving a high profile case such as this, they ended up at Rosie's with drinks all round until the early hours of the morning.

It was always a celebration accompanied by the euphoric feeling of having achieved something considerable. But this one was bitter-sweet. There would be no celebrations at Rosie's for solving this case.

Jack had spent many sleepless nights longing for the day, imagining how he would feel when he stopped this conceited killer who arrogantly taunted him with clues in a letter. But now he had his man, the feelings of satisfaction he expected to experience were replaced with a heavy weight in his gut and a stabbing pain through his heart.

The hardest part of all this won't be telling his colleagues, or his bosses, that he would get over with time. After all, in their eyes, Jack has still solved a major high profile case, regardless of who the killer was. The part about this whole situation he dreaded the most would be telling Max's mom what THEIR son had done and why he did it.

Jack's attention was drawn to Spence entering the office with two hot coffees. 'You looked like you could do with one of these Jobs,' Spence said as he placed a cup in front of Jack before sliding into the visitor's chair.

'You are a lifesaver Spence,' Jack said. He lifted the hot beverage and took a sip.

'Did you get everything finished up at Rumson?' Spence said. He reclined back, crossed his legs as he sipped on his coffee.

'Nearly. I should have it all done by this Saturday,' Jack said. 'The boxes are being collected the following Tuesday. So there is only a couple of things to tidy up and it will all be ready to go.'

'You OK buddy...?' Spence asked.

Jack stared briefly at Spence before responding. He couldn't bring himself to share his discovery with his colleague. Spence had been shoulder-to-shoulder with him through the Cryptic Killer investigation and he deserved to know the truth. He deserved to know it was finally over but he couldn't do it. 'I've been better,' was all Jack could bring himself to say.

'Where are the boxes going...? Caitlyn's...?'

'Yeah.' Jack nodded, sneaking in a quick sip of coffee. 'Eventually she'll go through them and sort out what she wants to keep and what to throw out but it will be a while before she can bring herself to doing that.'

'Well, sing out if you need a hand on Saturday, Jobs...' Spence offered.

Jack nodded as he sipped on his coffee.

Saturday was a cool overcast day and the evening was even cooler. The salty breeze blowing straight off the ocean made the temperatures feel about ten degrees cooler. Jack stood in the back yard of Max's Rumson house. His hands were shoved deep into his pockets and his hoodie was draped over his head.

He stared, mesmerized by the flames from the fire he had started in the tin drum. He momentarily enjoyed the warmth radiating from the dancing flames. A cardboard box lay at his feet. The words "PROPERTY OF JACK HEAD" were clearly visible across the top.

Jack was hypnotized by the flickering movement of the flames while his feelings and obligations as a father battled ferociously with his feelings and obligations as a career cop.

The decisions he made next could define him as a person; they could affect him for the rest of his life.

Jack loaded a further two small logs into the fire and stood back to watch the fire take hold. The heat radiating from the flames had a calming effect and provided him with some comfort from the cooler temperature.

The distinctive smell of burning logs mixed with the plumes of white smoke trailing off at a forty-five degree angle into the darkness.

Jack knelt down beside the box and ripped off the strong duct tape. He levered open the top flaps and peered inside the box. He paused briefly before reaching inside.

First to be removed from the box were the blank pages of lemon yellow paper and the envelopes. Jack paused briefly, mainly to reassure himself. He separated small groups of the pages then gently lobbed the blank pages and envelopes onto the fire. Within seconds the hungry flames stretched skywards.

The scrunched up newspaper articles all about Jack, followed next and were no match to the insatiable appetite of Jack's fire. The intense heat scorched them before they burst into flames and disintegrated into ash.

Jack reached into a pocket of his jeans and removed the small mobile phone SIM card and threw it straight into the fire. There was no hesitation. The fire's intense heat transformed the SIM into a molten blob of plastic in seconds.

He continued emptying the contents of the box, one-by-one until the empty shell of the box was all that remained. He stepped back and watched the flickering flames devour everything he had fed it.

He reached into his jeans back pocket and removed the folded autopsy report he received from the Long Beach cops. He opened it up and looked at it. He read the name across the top of the report –MAX JACK HEAD. He couldn't read any more. He shook his head as he crushed the report between his massive hands, scrunching it up tightly into a little ball. It was though he tried to squeeze any semblance of truth from it.

He watched as it exploded into flames after he lobbed it into the center of the fire drum.

Everything Jack had stumbled across in Max's basement that implicated Max as the Cryptic Killer was now reduced to ash. The only non-combustible item that remained was Max's laptop but he will wipe the hard drive then destroy it.

Jack's facial expression firmed. His eyebrows rose as he tapped the back pocket of his jeans. He suddenly remembered something. He removed a folded piece of paper. It was Max's confession letter to his mom.

He regarded the folded letter in his hand, deciding whether or not to burn it. Should he show it to Caitlyn? Would she want to see her son's last written words to her? Jack shook his head. He didn't know what to do. He decided to return it to his pocket for now.

Jack had just done the unthinkable. He had perverted the course of justice. He had tampered with evidence in a murder case, destroying it completely. Evidence that would have irrefutably identified the Cryptic Killer. Evidence from a man who murdered three young women and who attempted to kill another, was now gone, nothing but blackened ash in the bottom of the tin drum.

Jack stared at the mesmerizing flames that had devoured Max's incriminating evidence. The battle in his head over his obligations as a cop and a dad, the battle between right and wrong had been won. His protective obligations as a father and his feelings to protect his ex-wife had prevailed.

He had broken his oath to uphold the law. His actions questioned his integrity and went against everything he stood for. If caught, he would certainly be jailed for such an irresponsible and serious breach of trust. But he had to do it. He couldn't expose Max's mother to the additional grief of knowing her son was a serial killer.

His focus remained on the fire, mesmerized at its hypnotic beauty and comforting warmth, so much so, he didn't hear anyone approaching him from behind.

Jack startled when Spence placed his hand on his shoulder. He jumped and turned aggressively with his fists raised, ready to defend himself. It was an action that would strike fear into any man.

Spence raised both his hands. 'Whoa big boy...It's just me...' He said grinning back at Jack and the intense reaction he received.

Jack's shoulders relaxed. His right eyebrow arched as he quickly shifted his focus back to the fire drum to ensure that all trace of what he had recently fed the fire was now gone.

'I knocked at the front door but there was no answer. I could smell smoke so I came around back. You were miles away Jobs. I called out to you as I crossed the yard. You OK?'

'Yeah, good Spence,' Jack said, although he was not happy to see friend at that particular time. 'What the fuck are you doing here? You just took ten years off me.'

'I thought we needed to talk Jobs, so I thought this was as a good a place as any. It's out of the way. Just you and me, so I came down to see ya... See how you were coping and while I was here I thought we could have a chat.'

'OK. Talk about what?' Jack asked.

Spence didn't answer straight away. Both men stood with their hands in their pockets staring at the flickering flames. The front of their bodies glowed in the dancing reflection of the fire.

'Uniform called me...' Spence began. 'Apparently they were having trouble reaching you on your cell...'

'Yeah...I had it turned off. Didn't want to be disturbed...' Jack said watching the flames.

'Hmmm. Apparently Emma & Wylie came into the station today to view the photo of Van den Berg. Emma was adamant he wasn't the guy who attacked her and Wylie later confirmed Van den Berg wasn't the "Bear" he loaned the cars to...but I suspect you already knew that...' Spence said.

Jack's curious gaze flicked to Spence. He frowned.

'When did you first realize Jobs...?' Spence said, keeping his focus on the fire.

'Realize what...?' Jack said. A lump formed in his throat.

Spence nudged the empty cardboard box towards Jack with his foot, before lifting his eyes back to Jack.

Jack's head lowered. His friend had caught him out. 'When did YOU realize?' Jack said. His tone was somber, probably even embarrassed.

'Not until the funeral,' Spence began. 'When I saw the recent photos of Max on the large screen at the funeral, I thought I was looking at the photo fit IDs of our killer. Max looked more like the photo fit than what Van den Berg did. His steely blue eyes, his large frame. Everything matched. It all started to come together.

Then there were the photos at the funeral of him being awarded EXPERT level in KRAV MAGA...Krav Maga Jack, the Israeli Security Special forces self-defense that teaches you how to immobilize an attacker, maybe even break their neck if you wanted to...' Spence said, raising suggestive eyebrows.

'Then they mentioned during his eulogy he held a degree in Criminology...' Spence held a firm glare on Jack. 'Such a qualification could provide an insider's knowledge of crime scenes... couldn't it...?'

Jack didn't respond to Spence's rhetorical questions. He stood silent and motionless. His head was bowed submissively. His large shoulders were rounded, almost conceding.

What he had done was wrong and he couldn't justifiably
defend it. It didn't matter to the law that he did what he did
to protect his son's name and prevent further trauma to his
ex-wife.

'Then you came down here to pack Max's property and it was
obvious to me you found something,' Spence said. 'You
completely changed at work. You started conducting your
own separate inquiries, excluding me.

'You stopped your daily ritual of studying the whiteboard,
which suggested to me you knew something. I ran into Roger
in the kitchen and he asked how you went with the files on
Max's laptop.

'I thought to myself, why were you so interested in Max's
computer? There were a number of questions that needed
answering. So i thought I'd come down here and chat about
it all. But you just asked me when did I realize, Jack...?
When did I suspect we were looking at Max..? Just now. I
previously suspected something was up...I had no idea... but
I realized JUSTNOW.'

Jack was busted. His friend and partner, one of the most
trusted and loyal cops he knew had caught him doing the
unthinkable. Spence had caught him destroying
incriminating evidence in a multiple murder case.

Jack removed Max's letter from his pocket and handed it to
Spence. No words were exchanged. He didn't even look at
Spence, he just held the letter out in his extended hand.

Spence accepted the letter, unfolded it and read it to himself.
When he finished reading his stern glare flicked to Jack. His

eyebrows were raised. He held the letter out at Jack, holding his firm gaze for several seconds. Jack was too humiliated to bring himself to raise his head and make eye contact with Spence.

'How long have you had this...?' Spence shook the letter at Jack. He sounded disappointed that he was never told.

'Found it last weekend,' Jack said with his head still lowered. 'So...what happens now...?' Jack asked. His head was bowed in submission. His large shoulders were still rounded slightly.

Spence held his glare at Jack's lowered head without speaking. His face had firmed. He again held up the letter to Jack. 'This is a confession Jack,' he said directly. 'This is admissible evidence to identify who killed those three girls.' Jack remained unmoved. 'This will solve the Cryptic Killer case Jack...and it will also identify who attacked Emma Fisher,' he added firmly with his gaze still fixed on Jack. 'This is everything we have been looking for to identify the killer and solve the case...' Jack was unmoved.

After a brief pause Spence stepped to the fire. He took hold of the letter by the top corner and dipped the letter into the flickering flame until the bottom of the letter ignited.

The flame slowly climbed up the page. He tilted the letter to encourage the climbing flame, waiting until the last possible moment before tossing the fully engulfed page into the fire.

Spence stepped back from the fire and turned to face Jack. Jack's lowered head shot up. His eyes flicked from Spence to the fire and back.

'What happens now...?' Spence repeated. 'You asked me what happens now...I'll tell you what happens now... There's a killer out there somewhere and we don't know who it is.' Spence said. A wry grin filled Spence's face as he continued. 'We've got someone out there sending us cryptic letters Jack and running around killing hookers...and we have no idea who it is. We have no evidence on him and we gotta try and stop him. If we can't find him it will become a cold case and we will eventually move on. So to answer your question...' Spence placed a comforting hand on his friend's shoulder. 'That's what happens now. Not to mention that you've also got one son that you NEED to get to know and an ex-wife who I think would be keen on a second shot.'

Jack was overcome with emotion. His head dropped. He silently stared at the dancing flames that had consumed the last of Max's incriminating evidence. He gave an almost indiscernible shake of his head as tears welled up in his eyes at his friend's undeniable loyalty.

For years this tough, unbreakable giant was not allowed to show emotion. He wouldn't allow himself show emotion. His father taught him it was a sign of weakness. For years it was beaten into him that REAL MEN don't cry. This tough six foot eight, broad shouldered, old-school cop stood with his friend's supporting hand still resting on his shoulder, while a single tear over flowed and slowly trickled its pathway down his cheek.

The End

I hope you like this book soo please commnet and give review this book

THANK YOU